out of print
$10.00

THE WASHOE GIANT IN SAN FRANCISCO

The WASHOE GIANT IN SAN FRANCISCO

BEING HERETOFORE UNCOLLECTED SKETCHES

BY MARK TWAIN

PUBLISHED IN THE *GOLDEN ERA* IN THE SIXTIES INCLUDING *THOSE BLASTED CHILDREN, THE LICK HOUSE BALL, THE KEARNY STREET GHOST STORY, FITZ SMYTHE'S HORSE,* AND THIRTY-FOUR MORE ITEMS BY THE WILD HUMORIST OF THE PACIFIC SLOPE. WITH MANY DRAWINGS *by Lloyd Hoff.* COLLECTED AND EDITED, WITH AN INTRODUCTION

by Franklin Walker

FOLCROFT LIBRARY EDITIONS / 1973

Library of Congress Cataloging in Publication Data

Clemens, Samuel Langhorne, 1835-1910.
The Washoe giant in San Francisco.

Reprint of the ed. published by G. Fields, San Francisco.
Bibliography: p.
I. Walker, Franklin Dickerson, 1900- ed.
II. Golden era. III. Title.
PS1302.W3 1973 818'.4'07 73-8919
ISBN 0-8414-2683-X (lib. bdg.)

Limited 150 Copies

Manufactured in the United States of America.

The WASHOE GIANT IN SAN FRANCISCO

BEING HERETOFORE UNCOLLECTED SKETCHES

BY MARK TWAIN

PUBLISHED IN THE *GOLDEN ERA* IN THE SIXTIES INCLUDING *THOSE BLASTED CHILDREN, THE LICK HOUSE BALL, THE KEARNY STREET GHOST STORY, FITZ SMYTHE'S HORSE,* AND THIRTY-FOUR MORE ITEMS BY THE WILD HUMORIST OF THE PACIFIC SLOPE. WITH MANY DRAWINGS *by Lloyd Hoff.* COLLECTED AND EDITED, WITH AN INTRODUCTION *by Franklin Walker*

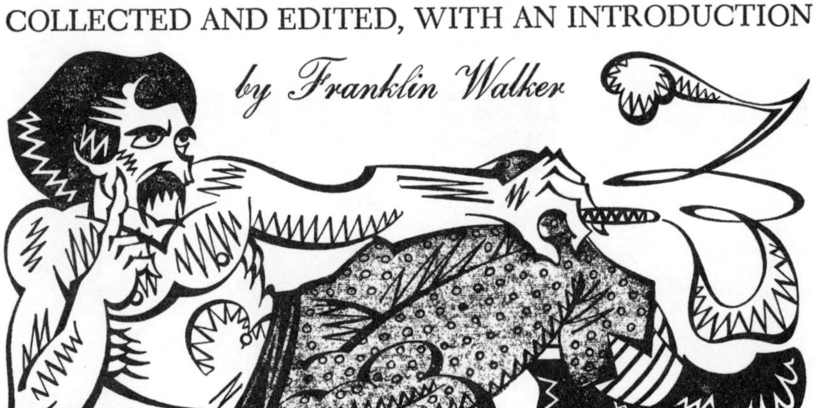

GEORGE FIELDS 1938 SAN FRANCISCO

TABLE OF CONTENTS

(Titles of forewords shown in italics)

INTRODUCTION

Mark Twain was dubbed the Washoe Giant because he arrived in San Francisco when the town was talking prize-fight. Two "boys" had just evaded the sheriff long enough to pound each other for forty rounds before a large group of sports assembled on the Contra Costa "picnic" grounds; and, consequently, Charles Henry Webb, better known as Inigo, used pugilism as his theme in writing his weekly column for the GOLDEN ERA. In it he challenged two celebrated visitors, Fitzhugh Ludlow and Mark Twain, to a journalistic battle, proposing an elimination contest between the Inigo Boy, the Hasheesh Infant and the Washoe Giant. The proposal then degenerated into bad puns, ending with the comment that "Inigo is bent on giving Ludlow Fitz, and rending apostolic Mark in Twain." Inigo would stop at nothing to make a pun; it was he who proposed a western epic opening with the line "arma virumque washoe"; who declared that Adah Isaacs Menken, in putting on the most famous strip-act of her day, was great in her line, but it was clearly not a clothesline; and who summed up the career of Sam Brannan, the self-elected Croesus of San Francisco, by calling him "a thing of booty and a bore forever." When he nicknamed precocious, bespectacled Fitzhugh Ludlow, youthful author of the notorious HASHEESH EATER, the Hasheesh Infant, he was no more timely than when he referred to Mark Twain as the Washoe Giant. Both names stuck.

To westerners Washoe was a much more familiar name than its polite superior, Nevada. The desert country that lay on the abrupt eastern slope of the Sierra, with its alkali flats and soda sinks lying many feet below but only a few miles distant from sparkling Tahoe, had been chistened Washoe by the emigrants of '49. The gold-seekers, wearily facing the last climb to California, compared the ribs of lava and the thatches of sage-brush in the wasteland to the hide and hair of the Washoe Indians, who lived on its piñon nuts and grasshoppers. As long as the county around Mt. Davidson was inhabited by Digger Indians, jack-rabbits, and the devil, it was Washoe, part of Utah. In 1860, however, when a bonanza was discovered in the mountain's flank, and Virginia City sprouted halfway up its barren side, the men who rushed back over the Sierra formed a new state and called it Nevada. But everyone still spoke of Washoe except when he was trying to be learned or formal.

Features of San Francisco life in the fall of 1863 were Washoe silver stocks, Washoe widows, and Washoe journalists. Nearly everyone was speculating in "feet" on the Comstock Lode, nearly as many were keeping Washoe widows from being too lonesome for their men across the mountain, and all who read newspapers had heard of the Virginia City TERRITORIAL ENTERPRISE's new humorist, Mark Twain. His was not a very old reputation, for he had been on the staff of the TERRITORIAL ENTERPRISE for only one year, had used the name Mark Twain for only six months.

Sam Clemens, ex-Mississippi river pilot, ex-Confederate soldier, spent an exciting but unremunerative winter mining in Unionville and Aurora before the opportunity came to substitute for the TERRITORIAL ENTERPRISE's feature writer, Dan De Quille, who had gone to the States for a year's vacation. Mark Twain soon made good. Readers in Washoe—and in San Francisco, which owned Washoe—recognized Mark Twain as the chap who wrote that hoax about the petrified man found thumbing his nose at the coroner, who carried on a friendly warfare with Rice of the Virginia City UNION, after naming him "The Unreliable," and who had quite recently made a stir with his gory account of the "Dutch Nick Massacre." Now that Dan De Quille had returned, Mark Twain was taking a short vacation in the city, getting a little of the applause and attention he deserved. In San Francisco he was a personage—the Washoe Giant. He wrote home from the Lick House: "I suppose I know at least a thousand people here—a great many of them citizens of San Francisco, but the majority belonging in Washoe—and when I go down Montgomery Street, it is just like being in

Main street in Hannibal and meeting the old familiar faces. I DO HATE *to go back to Washoe."* He drank beer at the Willows, he watched the seals from the Cliff House, and he even had a sail in the finest yacht on the Pacific Coast. In between times he made notes for the* GOLDEN ERA.

* * * *

THE GOLDEN ERA, *then in its twelfth year, was the livest literary sheet west of New York. Two youths, Rollin M. Daggett and J. Macdonough Foard, had founded the weekly in 1852, and with imagination and enterprise had sold it to miners from the Feather River to the Tuolumne, at the same time assuring themselves of generous support from San Francisco readers. Although the stories and poems at first had been almost all "selected", clipped from Eastern and European magazines in the day before copyright laws were general, gradually the chatty, informal eight-page journal succeeded in getting local writers to contribute to its columns. In the late fifties names like Old Block (Alonzo Delano), Yellow Bird (John R. Ridge), and Caxton (William H. Rhodes) appeared frequently in its pages. At the end of the decade the* GOLDEN ERA *gained a new lease on life by adding two new members to its staff. At the top, as editor, came urbane, witty, optimistic "Colonel" Joe Lawrence, famous for his tawny beard and meerschaum pipe; at the bottom, as compositor, was added Bret Harte, recently returned to San Francisco after three years of rustication near Eureka. Before the year was out Lawrence had published Harte's* M'LISS, *the first memorable story in American fiction to deal with the California frontier.*

Lawrence aimed at success for the GOLDEN ERA *with a double-barrelled program. With the left barrel he planned to get the best available local talent to work regularly for his paper, and with the right he hoped to persuade visitors of note to contribute during their stays in the West. His score on the local policy was almost perfect; it is no exaggeration to say that every western writer to attain prominence in the sixties and seventies, with the exceptions of Henry George and Ambrose Bierce, started his career on the* GOLDEN ERA. *Among others were Bret Harte, Charles Warren*

*Quoted from *Mark Twain's Letters,* Harper and Brothers, 1917. I; 90.

Stoddard, Ina Coolbrith, Joaquin Miller, Ralph Keeler, Frances Fuller Victor, and Prentice Mulford. Drawing his ammunition principally from Jerry Thomas's bar, Lawrence was equally effective in bagging visiting luminaries. Albert Bierstadt, the landscape artist, designed a new mast-head for the front page during his short stay on the coast; Fitzhugh Ludlow wrote for the paper while he was in San Francisco and continued sending in articles for months after his return to New York. Adah Isaacs Menken contributed many of her poems to its pages; Artemus Ward ran humorous sketches, as did Orpheus C. Kerr, the Civil War satirist; Ned Buntline wrote thrillers for it; and Ada Clare, Queen of Bohemia, was its columnist during her short and none too happy sojourn in California.

Even if Mark Twain had not been sure of an invitation to write for the GOLDEN ERA as a visitor of note, he would have been welcomed by Lawrence because of the close relationship between the Virginia City TERRITORIAL ENTERPRISE and the GOLDEN ERA. The GOLDEN ERA looked upon the TERRITORIAL ENTERPRISE as its child—or at least its younger brother. Both Joseph T. Goodman and Denis McCarthy, editors of the TERRITORIAL ENTERPRISE, had done their apprentice work on the GOLDEN ERA; Rollin M. Daggett, now local editor of the Nevada paper, had been one of the founders of the San Francisco journal; and Dan De Quille, humorist and mining expert for the TERRITORIAL ENTERPRISE, was the GOLDEN ERA's Virginia City correspondent. Mark Twain naturally drank a Pisco Punch with Colonel Lawrence and promised him his observations on fashions and politics while he was in the city. Thus the GOLDEN ERA was the first San Francisco journal to publish his writing.

* * * *

A year passed, however, before Mark Twain left Virginia City to live in San Francisco. The respite which he refers to in THE GREAT PRIZE FIGHT and THE LICK HOUSE BALL was followed by an extremely active winter in the sagebrush, a winter which started a little late with Artemus Ward's convivial visit, swung on through the meeting of the burlesque "Third House" in Carson City, and finished up in a whirl during the memorable campaign of selling and reselling a flour sack to raise money for the Sanitary Commission, the

Red Cross of the Civil War. The constant strain of horse-play, of practical jokes which were not always genially received, of burlesque feuds with other Virginia City journalists told on Mark's temper and furthered his restlessness. With gusto he had labeled Rice "The Unreliable" and yet had retained him as a close friend; with many a guffaw he pretended to wage war with his roommate, Dan De Quille, and yet he loved him; but ultimately fingers were burned, feelings riled in a tiff with Laird of the Virginia City UNION. Tradition, furthered by Steve Gillis's love for tall tales, has established the story that Mark Twain took the stage-coach out of Washoe because his quarrel with Laird passed the joking point. A minor fracas may have hurried the humorist on his way—although the story of a duel rests on questionable evidence—but Mark Twain had exhausted the opportunities of Virginia City and his time for departure had arrived. San Francisco was the next logical rung on the ladder. Everything in Virginia City from timber to banking, except the Washoe zephyr and the arsenic water, had been hauled over the ridge from California; and when a man made a strike on the Comstock his first thought was a palace on one of San Francisco's hills. There was a popular saying that Washoe people hoped to go to San Francisco rather than heaven when they died. Mark Twain's move was timely, for the flush days of the first Virginia City bonanza were over; hardly had he shaken the alkali dust from his boots before shares of Gould and Curry, the most substantial Comstock mine, dropped to a fraction of their boom value. The panic was on.

During the following two and one-half years, from May, 1864, to December, 1866, from the age of twenty-eight to thirty-one, Mark Twain lived in San Francisco. Even before this period he was a San Franciscan once removed. From the statement in ROUGHING IT that he had crossed the Sierra thirteen times we assume that he surely made three and possibly four trips to his new home before he left Nevada; hence, in passing from the mining town to the metropolis he was moving into a territory already partly conquered. As early as 1862 he associated himself with west-coast journalism, of which San Francisco was the focal point; as late as the summer of 1868, when he returned to arrange with the ALTA CALIFORNIA for the release of copyright on his QUAKER CITY letters, he looked upon himself as a roving correspondent with headquarters in California. Thus, during six of the years when Mark Twain's ideas and expression were taking form, he was addressing a San Franciscan audience.

Probably because the humorist had jumped from a small to a large puddle, the lover of Mark Twain anecdotes finds the San Francisco sojourn less interesting than the Virginia City stay. That hardly proves that it was less important. Because urban life was punctuated with escapades no more exciting than Steve Gillis's harrassing of his petulant friend with a "death-tick" rigged beneath his bed; than the efforts of the two companions to amuse themselves by throwing empty beer-bottles on the tin roofs of Chinese hovels; or than Mark Twain's attempt at civic reform when he borrowed a cabbage leaf from a vegetable vendor to fan, gravely and lingeringly, a policeman who had gone to sleep on his beat—because these incidents lack wildness it is nonsense to say that Mark Twain had struck a fallow period. Even if Charles Warren Stoddard was not as virile as Joseph T. Goodman, who had lamed a rival editor in a duel at Virginia City, there were still plenty of men in San Francisco who had used a gun and would use it again if necessary. But, as Joe Lawrence put it in the GOLDEN ERA, the city had matured enough to yield something better than silver bricks and mining feet, and "even Pegasus may freely roam when horse-stealing has become unpopular." During the sixties, before the railroad came to put an end to the isolation of the far-western frontier, a handful of writers—mostly San Francisco journalists—tried to express the spirit of a vanishing era. Mark Twain was for the moment one of them.

Readers familiar with Mark Twain's restlessness or with the limitation on the number of good places to live in San Francisco will not be surprised to hear that during his first four months in the city Mark tried two hotels and five lodging houses in order to get "comfortably fixed." As time went on he roamed even further in his search for ideas and comfort. He spent two winter months with Jim Gillis in his cabin on Jackass Hill and in nearby Angel's Camp heard Ross Coon drawl the story of the frog who lost the jumping contest because he was filled with bird-shot. He made frequent visits to Sacramento, San Jose, and Napa valley. He probably made at least one trip back to Washoe. During his last year on the coast he sailed on the new steamer AJAX to Honolulu as correspondent for the

SACRAMENTO UNION. *The success of his Sandwich Island letters suggested the trip to Europe which robbed California of Mark Twain but gave the world* INNOCENTS ABROAD.

Similarly, he moved from job to job, never seeming to find just what he wanted to write or to do. Two former connections with the San Francisco press were renewed as soon as he transferred from Virginia City to San Francisco; he again contributed weekly to the GOLDEN ERA *and he went on the staff of the San Francisco* CALL *as a city reporter. Although no biographer has pointed out an earlier connection with the* CALL, *the files indicate that Mark Twain had written Washoe correspondence for that journal during the fall of '63. He transferred his "literary work" from the* GOLDEN ERA *to the* CALIFORNIAN *in October, 1864, because of his conviction that Webb and Harte, both of whom had left the* ERA, *were printing a more "high-toned" journal than the miners' old favorite. His routine task on the* CALL, *a bustling, shrill, ineffective morning paper, was never to his liking, and, according to his story, after a few months of tiresome reporting he timed his resignation to anticipate his discharge. Only the need of money could have made him work for the* CALL *as long as he did; he went through a monotonous daily regime in getting local news, which were de-humanized before printing; he was allowed to sign no articles. Even the weekly drama review, which must have been his, shows no sign of his customary ways of thinking or writing.*

Soon after he left the CALL *he began writing a daily comment on San Francisco life for the Virginia City* TERRITORIAL ENTERPRISE, *a practice which he continued, at least intermittently, until he made the voyage to the Sandwich Islands. Albert Bigelow Paine in his biography of Mark Twain testified to the sensation that these articles created in California, but, because a complete file of the* TERRITORIAL ENTERPRISE *has not survived, he feared that the more interesting articles were irretrievably lost. Now for the first time they are given to the public—not directly from the* TERRITORIAL ENTERPRISE *but from the* GOLDEN ERA, *which made a policy of reprinting the cream of the Mark Twain correspondence. Thus we are able to learn from the original text how Mark Twain carried on a campaign against the police, how he pilloried "Fitz Smythe" of the* ALTA, *and how he investigated the doings of the spiritualists.*

In this series of GOLDEN ERA *sketches the items known to have appeared first in the* TERRITORIAL ENTERPRISE *are initialed "T. E."*

Through the pages of the GOLDEN ERA we follow Mark Twain up to March 7, 1866, the day that he sailed for Honolulu. When he returned from this voyage he was ready to go another step up the ladder. Already he had sold his first article to an Eastern magazine, and within a year his first book was to be released. In THE JUMPING FROG, AND OTHER SKETCHES he was to be introduced to the world as "The Wild Humorist of the Pacific Slope" with added comment that he would go down to posterity as "The Moralist of the Main." Before he left San Francisco he discovered his talents in one other direction by proving that he was a success as a lecturer. A full house at Maguire's Academy of Music listened to him deliver his lecture on the Sandwich Islands; old friends recognized the mop of reddish-brown hair, the dragging of one foot as he crossed the stage, the hesitant, awkward posture; those who had never seen him before were delighted with his drawl, his perturbed expression, and the surprised look following painful effort whenever his play took the trick. His triumphal procession took him through Sacramento, Marysville, Grass Valley, Nevada City, You Bet, Red Dog, Virginia City, Carson, Gold Hill, Silver Hill, and Dayton.

Mark Twain never had to look for a job again. When he returned from his lecture tour the proprietors of the ALTA CALIFORNIA, the oldest and most important San Francisco newspaper, offered to advance money to pay for a European tour. Mark Twain was to earn his way by portraying Old World culture as viewed by a frontiersman with a sense of humor. On December 15, 1866, he sailed for Nicaragua. The western frontier had given him all that he could use. It had taught him to write, it had taught him to speak; and, most important of all, it had contributed immeasurably to the way of thinking which was to make him great.

FRANKLIN WALKER.

I. THE WASHOE GIANT VISITS SAN FRANCISCO

Those BLASTED CHILDREN

BECAUSE MARK TWAIN CONSIDERED *"Those Blasted Children" to be a "pearl which ought for the eternal welfare of my race to have a more extensive circulation than is afforded by a local daily paper"* * *he sent it to the New York* SUNDAY MERCURY. *It is the earliest identified writing by Mark Twain to appear in an Eastern periodical. Its author apparently planned to use it as the title sketch of his first book and might have done so had not "The Jumping Frog of Calaveras County become the rage. Though the date 1864 stands at the head of the sketch, internal evidence shows that Mark Twain threw the bootjack at those blasted children during his stay at the* LICK HOUSE *in the summer of '63.*

Albert Bigelow Paine expressed relief that this sketch was never reprinted, stating that it was "scarcely refined in character and full of personal allusions"; in doing so, he was taking his stand with Ada Clare, the GOLDEN ERA *columnist with the blonde curls, who said that in it Mark Twain was "guilty of misunderstanding God's little people." The modern reader will let the children take care of themselves. Doubtless he will miss some good satire by not knowing all about the fathers of Flora Low and Florence Hillyer, but he will not have to be a student of California history to figure out that one was state governor and the other a Washoe nabob. He should be told, however, that Zeb Leavenworth, who testified that he cut off his son's lower jaw in an attempt to stop his stammering, was erstwhile pilot of the* JOHN R. ROE *on the Mississippi and helped to teach Sam Clemens the river. Doubtless Sam sent Zeb a copy as soon as it was off the press.*

* Quoted from a letter appearing in *Mark Twain, A Biography* by A. B. Paine, Harpers, 1912. pp. 243-244.

THOSE BLASTED CHILDREN

LICK HOUSE, San Francisco,
Wednesday, 1864.

NO. 165 IS A PLEASANT ROOM. It is situated at the head of a long hall, down which, on either side, are similar rooms occupied by sociable bachelors, and here and there one tenanted by an unsociable nurse or so. Charley Creed sleeps in No. 157. He is my timepiece—or, at least, his boots are. If I look down the hall and see Charley's boots still before his door, I know it is early yet, and I may hie me sweetly to bed again. But if those unerring boots are gone, I know it is after eleven o'clock, and time for me to be rising with the lark.

This reminds me of the lark of yesterday and last night which was altogether a different sort of bird from the one I am talking about now. Ah me! Summer girls and summer dresses, and summer scenes at the "Willows," Seal Rock Point, and the grim sea-lions wallowing in the angry surf; glimpses through the haze of stately ships far away at sea, a dash along the smooth beach, and the exhilaration of watching the white waves come surging ashore, and break into seething foam about the startled horse's feet; reveries beside the old wreck, half buried in sand, and compassion for the good ship's fate; home again in a soft twilight, oppressed with the odor of flowers—home again to San Francisco, drunk, perhaps, but not disorderly. Dinner at six, with ladies and gentlemen, dressed with faultless taste and elegance, and all drunk, apparently, but very quiet and well-bred—unaccountably so, under the circumstances, it seemed to my cloudy brain. Many things happened after that, I remember,—such as visiting some of their haunts with those dissipated Golden Era fellows, and—Here come those young savages again—those noisy and inevitable children. God be with them!—or they with him, rather, if it be not asking too much. They are another time-piece of mine. It is two o'clock now; they are invested with their regular lunch, and have come up here to settle it. I will soothe my troubled spirit with a short season of blasphemy, after which I will expose their infamous feelings with a relentless pen. They have driven me from labor many and many a time; but behold! the hour of retribution is at hand.

That is young Washington Billings, now—a little dog in long flaxen curls and Highland costume.

"Hi, Johnny! look through the keyhole! here's that feller with a long nose, writing again—less stir him up!" [A double kick against the door —a grand infant war-whoop in full chorus—and then a clatter of scampering feet down the echoing corridors.] Ah—one of them has fallen, and hurt himself. I hear the intelligent foreign nurse boxing his ears for it (the parents, Mr. and Mrs. Kerosene, having gone up to Sacramento on the evening boat, and left their offspring properly cared for.)

Here they come again, as soldiers—infantry. I know there are not more than thirty or forty of them, yet they are under no sort of discipline, and they make noise enough for a thousand. Young Oliver Higgins is in command. They assault my works—they try to carry my position by storm—they finally draw off with boisterous cheers, to harrass a handful of skirmishers thrown out by the enemy—a bevy of chambermaids.

Once more they come trooping down the hall. This time as cavalry. They must have captured and disarmed the skirmishers, for half my young ruffians are mounted on broomsticks. They make a reconnoissance in force. They attack my premises in a body, but they achieve nothing approaching a success. I am too strongly intrenched for them.

They invest my stronghold, and lay siege to it—that is to say, they sit down before my camp, and betake themselves to the pastimes of youth. All talking at once, as they do, their conversation is amusing, but not instructive to me:

"Ginn me some o' that you're eat'n." "I won't—you wouldn't lemme play with that dead rat, the peanut-boy give you yesterday." "Well! I don't care; I reckon I know summun't you don't; Oho, Mr. Smarty, 'n' I ain't a goin' to tell you, neither; now, see what you got by it; it's summun't my ma said about your ma, too. I'll tell you, if you'll gimme ever so little o' that, will you? Well." (I imagine from the break in this conversation, while the other besiegers go on talking noisily, that a compromise is being effected.) "There, don't take so much. Now, what'd she say?" "Why, ma told my pa't if your ma is so mighty rich now she wasn't nobody till she come to Sanf'cisco. That's what she said." "Your ma's a big story-teller, 'n' I'm goin' jes' as straight as I can walk, 'n' tell my ma. You'll see what she'll do." (I foresee a diversion in one or two family circles.) "Flora Low, you quit pulling that doll's legs out, it's mine." "Well, take your old doll, then. I'd thank you to know, Miss Florence Hillyer, 't my pa's Governor, 'n' I can have a thousan' dolls if I want to, 'n' gold ones, too, or silver, or anything." (More trouble brewing.) "What do I care for that. I guess my pa could be Governor, too, if he wanted to; but he don't. He owns two hundred feet in the Chollar, 'n' he's got lots more silver mines in Washoe besides. He could fill this house full of silver, clear up to that chandelier, so he could, now, Miss." "You, Bob Miller, you leg go that string—I'll smack you in the eye." "You will, will you? I'd like to see you try it. You jes' hit me if you dare!" "You lay your hands on me, 'n' I will hit you." "Now I've laid my hand on you, why don't you hit?" "Well, I mean, if you lay 'em on me so's to hurt." "Ah-h! you're afraid, that's the reason!" "No I ain't, neither, you big fool." (Ah, now they're at it. Discord shall invade the ranks of my foes, and they shall fall by their own hands. It appears from the sound without that two nurses have made a descent upon the combatants, and are bearing them from the field. The nurses are abusing each other. One boy proclaims that the other struck him when he wasn't doin' nothin'; and the other boy says he was called a big fool. Both are going right straight, and tell their pa's. Verily, things are going along as comfortably as I could wish, now.) "Sandy Baker, I know what makes your pa's hair kink so; it's 'cause he's a mulatter; I heard my ma say so." "It's a lie!" (Another row, and more skirmishing with the nurses. Truly, happiness flows in upon me most bountifully this day.)

Hi, boys! here comes a Chinaman. (God pity any Chinaman who chances to come in the way of the boys hereabouts, for the eye of the law regardeth him not, and the youth of California in their generation are down upon him.) Now, boys! grab his clothes basket—take him by the tail! (There they go, now, like a pack of young demons; they have confiscated the basket, and the dismayed Chinaman is towing half the tribe down the hall by his cue. Rejoice, O my soul, for behold, all things are lovely, etc.—to speak after the manner of the vulgar.) "Oho, Miss Susy Badger, my uncle Tom's goin' across the bay to Oakland, 'n' down to Santa Clara, 'n' Alamedy, 'n' San Leandro, 'n' everywheres—all over the world, 'n' he's goin' to take me with him—he said so." "Humph! that ain't noth'n—I been there. My aunt Mary'd take me to any place I wanted to go, if I wanted her to, but I don't; she's got horses 'n' things —O, ever so many!—millions of 'em; but my ma says it don't look well for little girls to be always gadd'n about. That's why you don't ever see me goin' to places like some girls do. I despise to—" (The end is at hand; the nurses have massed themselves on the left; they move in serried phalanx on my besiegers; they surround them, and capture the last miscreant—horse, foot, and dragoons, munitions of war, and camp equipage. The victory is complete. They are gone—my castle is no longer menaced, and the rover is free. I am here, staunch and true!)

It is a living wonder to me that I haven't scalped some of those children before now. I expect I would have done it, but then I hardly felt well enough acquainted with them. I scarcely ever show them any attention anyhow, unless it is to throw a bootjack at them or some little nonsense of that kind when I happen to feel playful. I am confident I would have destroyed several of them though, only it might appear as if I were making most too free

I observe that that young officer of the Pacific squadron—the one with his nostrils turned up like port-holes—has become a great favorite with half the mothers in the house, by imparting to them much useful information concerning the manner of doctoring children among the South American savages. His brother is brigadier in the Navy. The drab-complexioned youth with the Solferino mustache has corralled the other half with the Japanese treatment.—The more I think of it, the more I admire it. Now, I am no peanut. I have an idea that I could invent some little remedies that would stir up a commotion among these women, if I chose to try. I always had a good general notion of physic, I believe. It is one of my natural gifts, too, for I have never studied a single day under a regular physician. I will jot down a few items here, just to see how likely I am to succeed.

In the matter of measles, the idea is, to bring it out—bring it to the surface. Take the child and fill it up with saffron tea. Add something to make the patient sleep—say a table-spoonful of arsenic. Don't rock it, it will sleep anyhow.

As far as brain fever is concerned: This is a very dangerous disease. and must be treated with decision and dispatch. In every case where it has proved fatal, the sufferer invariably perished. You must strike at the root of the distemper. Remove the brains; and then— Well, that will be sufficient—that will answer—just remove the brains. This remedy has never been known to fail. It was invented by the lamented J. W. Macbeth, Thane of Cawdor, Scotland, who refers to it thus: "Time was, that when the brains were out, the man would die; but, under different circumstances, I think not; and, all things being equal, I believe you, my boy." Those were his last words.

Concerning worms: Administer a catfish three times a week. Keep the room very quiet; the fish won't bite if there is the least noise.

When you come to fits, take no chances on fits. If the child has them bad, soak it in a barrel of rain water over night, or a good article of vinegar. If this does not put an end to its troubles, soak it a week. You can't soak a child too much when it has fits.

In cases wherein an infant stammers, remove the under-jaw. In proof of the efficacy of this treatment, I append the following certificate, voluntarily forwarded to me by Mr. Zeb. Leavenworth, of St. Louis, Mo.:

St. Louis, May 26, 1863.

"Mr. Mark Twain—*Dear Sir:*—Under Providence, I am beholden to you for the salvation of my Johnny. For a matter of three years, that suffering child stuttered to that degree that it was a pain and a sorrow to me to hear him stagger over the sacred name of 'p-p-p-pap.' It troubled me so that I neglected my business; I refused food; I took no pride in my dress, and my hair began to actually fall off. I could not rest; I could not sleep. Morning, noon, and night, I did nothing but moan pitifully, and murmur to myself: 'Hell's fire, what am I going to do about my Johnny?' But in a blessed hour you appeared unto me like an angel from the skies; and without hope of reward, revealed your sovereign remedy—and that very day, I sawed off my Johnny's under-jaw. May Heaven bless you, noble Sir. It afforded instant relief; and my Johnny has never stammered since. I honestly believe he never will again. As to disfigurement, he does seem to look sorter ornery and hog-mouthed, but I am too grateful in having got him effectually saved from that dreadful stuttering, to make much account of small matters. Heaven speed you in your holy work of healing the afflictions of humanity. And if my poor testimony can be of any service to you, do with it as you think will result in the greatest good to our fellow creatures. Once more, Heaven bless you.

Zeb. Leavenworth."

Now, that has such a plausible ring about it, that I can hardly keep from believing it myself. I consider it a very fair success.

Regarding cramps. Take your offspring—let the same be warm and dry at the time—and immerse it in a commodious soup-tureen filled with the best quality of camphene. Place it over a slow fire, and add reasonable quantities of pepper, mustard, horse-radish, saltpetre, strychnine, blue vitrol, aqua fortis, a quart of flour, and eight or ten fresh eggs, stirring it from time to time, to keep up a healthy reaction. Let it simmer fifteen minutes. When your child is done, set the tureen off, and allow the infallible remedy to cool. If this does not confer an entire insensibility to cramps you must lose no time, for the case is desperate.

Take your offspring, and parboil it. The most vindictive cramps cannot survive this treatment; neither can the subject, unless it is endowed with an iron constitution. It is an extreme measure, and I always dislike to resort to it. I never parboil a child until everything else has failed to bring about the desired end.

Well, I think those will do to commence with. I can branch out, you know, when I get more confidence in myself.

O infancy! thou art beautiful, thou art charming, thou art lovely to contemplate! But thoughts like these recall sad memories of the past, of the halcyon days of my childhood, when I was a sweet, prattling innocent, the pet of a dear home-circle and the pride of the village.

Enough, enough! I must weep, or this bursting heart will break.

FROM THE *Golden Era, March 27, 1864*
REPRINTED FROM THE *New York Sunday Mercury.*

The

GREAT PRIZE FIGHT

IN "THE GREAT PRIZE FIGHT" *Mark Twain scored a triple, capitalizing on the prize-fight excitement, taking a few digs at the politicians, and creating a situation in which he could tell how one man hauled out another man's left lung and smacked him in the face with it. Prize-fight procedure and prize-fight vocabulary invited burlesque. An issue of the California* POLICE GAZETTE *gives detail on a fight of the period. A large crowd of sportsmen, transported in a special train to a "picnic" down the peninsula, expressed delight and surprise at finding a ring rigged in a meadow and Chandler and Harris ready for a go without gloves. When the sheriff intervened, the show was called off for the day, but the whole crowd set off in boats the next morning, ostensibly headed for Sausalito but actually for a point on the Contra Costa shore nine miles north of Oakland. The fight went twenty-three rounds before Harris quit with a broken jaw and three teeth knocked out. After the main event, two local boys fought through one hundred and six rounds before darkness stopped the encounter.*

The account of the fight in the POLICE GAZETTE *outdoes modern sport jargon in vigor and metaphor. "Dooney comes up fresh, but bleeding from hash trap and bugle. He strikes out for Chandler, whom he hits heavily on the kisser, but receives it good on the sconce in return." Bret Harte burlesqued the language in a poem called "The Prize Fighter to his Mistress," published in the* GOLDEN ERA *on the same day "The Great Prize Fight" appeared. It contains lines such as*

> *"But bid him behold thy dear 'mug' on this breast,*
> *This 'bunch of fives' clasping thy own lovely 'fin'."*

But he could not fetch the tune as well as Mark Twain.

Shortly before this sketch appeared, Low had been elected governor of California to succeed Stanford; both men were Republicans, but

Stanford had withdrawn from the convention when he saw that the party chiefs favored his opponent. The reader will need no introduction to the capable sponge-holders, Stephen J. Field and Wm. M. Stewart, supreme court judge and future senator from Nevada, respectively; Brigadier General Wright was in military command of the West during this period of the Civil War. Finally, the "Greek Slave" was Hiram Powers' famous statue of a naked girl, the "September Morn" of its period, which furnished journalists with a subject for countless allusions.

THE ONLY TRUE AND RELIABLE ACCOUNT OF

THE GREAT PRIZE FIGHT

For $100,000 at

SEAL ROCK POINT, ON SUNDAY LAST,

BETWEEN HIS EXCELLENCY GOV. STANFORD AND HON. F. F. LOW, GOVERNOR ELECT OF CALIFORNIA.

FOR THE PAST MONTH the sporting world has been in a state of feverish excitement on account of the grand prize fight set for last Sunday between the two most distinguished citizens of California, for a purse of a hundred thousand dollars. The high social standing of the competitors, their exalted position in the arena of politics, together with the princely sum of money staked upon the issue of the combat, all conspired to render the proposed prize-fight a subject of extraordinary importance, and to give it an eclat never before vouchsafed to such a circumstance since the world began. Additional lustre was shed upon the coming contest by the lofty character of the seconds or bottle-holders chosen by the two champions, these being no other than Judge Field (on the part of Gov. Low), Associate Justice of the Supreme Court of the United States, and Hon. Wm. M. Stewart, (commonly called "Bill Stewart," or "Bullyragging Bill Stewart,") of the city of Virginia, the most popular as well as the most distinguished lawyer in Nevada Territory, member of the Constitutional Convention, and future U. S. Senator for the State of Washoe, as I hope and believe—on the part of Gov. Stanford. Principals and seconds together, it is fair to presume that such an array of talent was never entered for a combat of this description upon any previous occasion.

Stewart and Field had their men in constant training at the Mission during the six weeks preceding the contest, and such was the interest taken in the matter that thousands visited that sacred locality daily to pick up such morsels of information as they might, concerning the physical and scientific improvement being made by the gubernatorial acrobats. The anxiety manifested by the populace was intense. When it was learned that Stanford had smashed a barrel of flour to atoms with a single blow of his fist, the voice of the people was on his side. But when the news came that Low had caved in the head of a tubular boiler with one stroke of his powerful "mawley" (which term is in strict accordance with the language of the ring,) the tide of opinion changed again. These changes were frequent, and they kept the minds of the public in such a state of continual vibration that I fear the habit thus acquired is confirmed, and that they will never more cease to oscillate.

The fight was to take place on last Sunday morning at ten o'clock. By nine every wheeled vehicle and every species of animal capable of bearing burthens, were in active service, and the avenues leading to the Seal Rock swarmed with them in mighty processions whose numbers no man might hope to estimate.

I determined to be upon the ground at an early hour. Now I dislike to be exploded, as it were, out of my balmy slumbers, by a sudden, stormy assault upon my door, and an imperative order to "Get up!"—wherefore I requested one of the intelligent porters of the Lick House to call at my palatial apartments, and murmur gently through the keyhole the magic monosyllable "Hash!" That "fetched me."

The urbane livery-stable keeper furnished me with a solemn, short-bodied, long-legged animal—a sort of animated counting-house stool, as it were—which he called a "Morgan" horse. He told me who the brute was "sired" by, and was proceeding to tell me who he was "dammed" by, but I gave him to understand that I was competent to damn the horse myself, and should probably do it very effectually before I got to the battle-ground. I mentioned to him, however, that as I was not proposing to attend a funeral, it was hardly necessary to furnish me an animal gifted with such oppressive solemnity of bearing as distinguished his "Morgan." He said in reply, that Morgan was only pensive when in the stable, but that on the road I would find him one of the liveliest horses in the world.

He enunciated the truth.

The brute "bucked" with me from the foot of Montgomery street to the Occidental Hotel. The laughter which he provoked from the crowds of citizens along the side-walks, he took for applause, and honestly made every effort in his power to deserve it, regardless of consequences.

He was very playful, but so suddenly were the creations of his fancy conceived and executed, and so much ground did he take up with them, that it was safest to behold them from a distance. In the selfsame moment of time, he shot his heels through the side of a street-car, and then backed himself into Barry and Patten's and sat down on the free-lunch table.

Such was the length of this Morgan's legs.

Between the Occidental and the Lick House, having become thoroughly interested in his work, he planned and carried out a series of the most extraordinary maneuvers ever suggested by the brain of any horse. He arched his neck and went tripping daintily across the street sideways, "rairing up" on his hind legs occasionally, in a very disagreeable way, and looking into the second-story windows. He finally waltzed into the large ice cream saloon opposite the Lick House, and——

But the memory of that perilious voyage hath caused me to digress from the proper subject of this paper, which is the great prize-fight between Governors Low and Stanford. I will resume.

After an infinitude of fearful adventures, the history of which would fill many columns of this newspaper, I finally arrived at the Seal Rock Point at a quarter to ten—two hours and a half out from San Francisco, and not less gratified than surprised that I ever got there at all—and anchored my noble Morgan to a boulder on the hill-side. I had to swathe his head in blankets also, because, while my back was turned for a single moment, he developed another atrocious trait of his most remarkable character. He tried to eat little Augustus Maltravers Jackson, the "humbly" but interesting off-spring of Hon. J. Belvidere Jackson, a wealthy barber from San Jose. It would have been a comfort to me to leave the infant to his fate, but I did not feel able to pay for him.

When I reached the battle-ground, the great champions were already stripped and prepared for the "mill." Both were in splendid condition, and displayed a redundancy of muscle about the breast and arms which was delightful to the eye of the sportive connoisseur. They were well matched. Adepts said that Stanford's "heft" and tall stature were fairly offset by Low's superior litheness and activity. From their heads to the Union colors around their waists, their costumes were similar to that of the Greek Slave; from thence down they were clad in flesh-colored tights and grenadier boots.

The ring was formed upon the beautiful level sandy beach above the Cliff House, and within twenty paces of the snowy surf of the broad Pacific ocean, which was spotted here and there with monstrous sea-lions attracted shoreward by curiosity concerning the vast multitudes of people collected in the vicinity.

At five minutes past ten, Brigadier General Wright, the Referee, notified the seconds to bring their men "up to the scratch." They did so, amid the shouts of the populace, the noise whereof rose high above the roar of the sea.

First Round.—The pugilists advanced to the centre of the ring, shook hands, retired to their respective corners, and at the call of the time-keeper, came forward and went at it. Low dashed out handsomely with his left and gave Stanford a paster in the eye, and at the same moment his adversary mashed him in the ear. [These singular phrases are entirely proper, Mr. Editor—I find them in the copy of "Bell's Life in London" now lying before me.] After some beautiful sparring, both parties went down—that is to say, they went down to the bottle-holders. Stewart and Field, and took a drink.

Second Round.—Stanford launched out a well intended plunger, but Low parried it admirably and instantly busted him in the snoot. [Cries of "Bully for the Marysville Infant!"] After some lively fibbing (both of them are used to it in political life) the combatants went to grass. [See "Bell's Life."]

Third Round.—Both came up panting considerably. Low let go a terrific side-winder, but Stanford stopped it handsomely and replied with an earthquake on Low's bread-basket. [Enthusiastic shouts of "Sock it to him, my Sacramento Pet!"] More fibbing—both down.

Fourth Round.—The men advanced and sparred warily for a few moments, when Stanford exposed his cocoanut an instant, and Low struck out from the shoulder and split him in the mug. [Cries of "Bully for the Fat Boy!"]

Fifth Round.—Stanford came up looking wicked, and let drive a heavy blow with his larboard flipper which caved in the side of his adversary's head. [Exclamations of "Hi! at him again Old Rusty!"]

From this time until the end of the conflict, there was nothing regular in the proceedings. The two champions got furiously angry, and used up each other thus:

No sooner did Low realize that the side of his head was crushed in like a dent in a plug hat, than he "went after" Stanford in the most desperate manner. With one blow of his fist he mashed his nose so far into his face that a cavity was left in its place the size and shape of an ordinary soup-bowl. It is scarcely necessary to mention that in making room for so much nose, Gov. Stanford's eyes were crowded to such a degree as to cause them to "bug out" like a grasshopper's. His face was so altered that he scarcely looked like himself at all.

I never saw such a murderous expression as Stanford's countenance now assumed; you see it was so concentrated—it had such a small number of features to spread around over. He let fly one of his battering rams and caved in the other side of Low's head. Ah me, the latter was a ghastly sight to contemplate after that—one of the boys said it looked "like a beet which somebody had trod on it."

Low was "grit" though. He dashed out with his right and stove Stanford's chin clear back even with his ears. Oh, what a horrible sight he was, gasping and reaching after his tobacco, which was away back among his under-jaw teeth.

Stanford was unsettled for a while, but he soon rallied, and watching his chance, aimed a tremendous blow at his favorite mark, which crushed in the rear of Gov. Low's head in such a way that the crown thereof projected over his spinal column like a shed.

He came up to the scratch like a man, though, and sent one of his ponderous fists crashing through his opponent's ribs and in among his vitals, and instantly afterward he hauled out poor Stanford's left lung and smacked him in the face with it.

If ever I saw an angry man in my life it was Leland Stanford. He fairly raved. He jumped at his old speciality, Gov. Low's head; he tore it loose from his body and knocked him down with it. [Sensation in the crowd.]

Staggered by his extraordinary exertion, Gov. Stanford reeled, and before he could recover himself the headless but indomitable Low sprang forward, pulled one of his legs out by the roots, and dealt him a smashing paster over the eye with the end of it. The ever watchful Bill Stewart sallied out to the assistance of his crippled principal with a pair of crutches, and the battle went on again as fiercely as ever.

At this stage of the game the battle ground was strewn with a sufficiency of human remains to furnish material for the construction of three or four men of ordinary size, and good sound brains enough to stock a whole country like the one I came from in the noble old state of Missouri. And so dyed were the combatants in their own gore that they looked like shapeless, mutilated, red-shirted firemen.

The moment a chance offered, Low grabbed Stanford by the hair of the head, swung him thrice round and round in the air like a lasso, and then slammed him on the ground with such mighty force that he quivered all over, and squirmed painfully, like a worm; and behold, his body and such of his limbs as he had left, shortly assumed a swollen aspect like unto those of a rag doll-baby stuffed with saw-dust.

He rallied again, however, and the two desperadoes clinched and never let up until they had minced each other into such insignificant odds and ends that neither was able to distinguish his own remnants from those of his antagonist. It was awful.

Bill Stewart and Judge Field issued from their corners and gazed upon the sanguinary reminiscences in silence during several minutes. At the end of that time, having failed to discover that either champion had got the best of the fight, they threw up their sponges simultaneously, and Gen. Wright proclaimed in a loud voice that the battle was "drawn." May my ears never again be rent asunder with a burst of sound similar to that which greeted this announcement, from the multitude. Amen.

By order of Gen. Wright, baskets were procured, and Bill Stewart and Judge Field proceeded to gather up the fragments of their late principals, while I gathered up my notes and went after my infernal horse, who had slipped his blankets and was foraging among the neighboring children. I— * * * * * * *

P. S.—Messrs. Editors, I have been the victim of an infamous hoax. I have been imposed upon by that ponderous miscreant, Mr. Frank Lawler, of the Lick House. I left my room a moment ago, and the first man I met on the stairs was Gov. Stanford, alive and well, and as free from mutilation as you or I. I was speechless. Before I reached the street, I actually met Gov. Low also, with his own head on his own shoulders, his limbs intact, his inner mechanism in its proper place, and his cheeks blooming with gorgeous robustitude. I was amazed. But a word of explanation from him convinced me that I had been swindled by Mr. Lawler with a detailed account of a fight which had never occurred, and was never likely to occur; that I had believed him so implicitly as to sit down and write it out (as other reporters have done before me) in language calculated to deceive the public into the conviction that I was present at it myself, and to embellish it with a string of falsehoods intended to render that deception as plausible as possible.

I ruminated upon my singular position for many minutes, arrived at no conclusion—that is to say, no satisfactory conclusion, except that Lawler was an accomplished knave and I was a consummate ass. I had suspected the first before, though, and been acquainted with the latter fact for nearly a quarter of a century.

In conclusion, permit me to apologise in the most abject manner to the present Governor of California, to Hon. Mr. Low, the Governor-elect, to Judge Field and to Hon. Wm. M. Stewart, for the great wrong which my natural imbecility has impelled me to do them in penning and publishing the foregoing sanguinary absurdity. If it were to do over again, I don't really know that I would do it. It is not possible for me to say how I ever managed to believe that refined and educated gentlemen like these could stoop to engage in the loathsome and degrading pastime of prize-fighting. It was just Lawler's work, you understand—the lubberly, swelled-up effigy of a nine-days drowned man! But I shall get even with him for this. The only excuse he offers is that he got the story from John B. Winters, and thought of course it must be just so—as if a future Congressman for the State of Washoe could by any possibility tell the truth! Do you know that if either of these miserable scoundrels were to cross my path while I am in this mood I would scalp him in a minute? That's me—that's my style.

FROM THE *Golden Era*, OCT. 11, 1863.

The

LICK HOUSE BALL

AND OTHER FASHION REVIEWS

THE RIDICULOUS SOCIETY reviews which appeared in the local press after each important ball of the season were as tempting to a humorist as an Eton hat to an American boy with a snow-ball. Sally Sorrell or Occasia Owen would go through the list of well-known ladies present, and, after mentioning each by initials, would say something nice about what she wore. Thus, the "serious" write-up of the Lick House Ball read as follows: "Mrs. Hon. F. F. L.—wore a dark pink silk beautifully and tastefully trimmed with black lace; the arrangement of her hair was faultless, and the ornaments neat and APROPOS. She was beautiful and capitivating . . . the 'fairest of the fair.' Miss F——d was dressed in a plain sky-blue silk. She danced as gracefully and seemed as charming as ever. Mrs. F. J——n looked exquisitely. Her dress was a light pink MOIRE ANTIQUE; hair artistically arranged in puffs" et cetera ad nauseam. Mark Twain could not resist the temptation to play with the initials, mimic the trite phrases, and burlesque the foreign names for materials and styles. After delighting the Washoe socialites with a burlesque society review in the TERRITORIAL ENTERPRISE, he was called upon to repeat the performance several times in San Francisco.

Although I am aware that this sort of travesty soon palls, I have included all of the fashion reviews not reprinted elsewhere hoping that the reader will search through the chaff to find the occasional grain. There are some good remarks to be noted; one would regret missing the "tasteful tarantula done in jet" or the "gorgeous bouquet of real sagebrush imported from Washoe" which rested on Mrs. J. B. W.'s bosom. I have salvaged a diatribe directed at Miss X omitted from the book-printing of "The Pioneers' Ball" and also a stray item on the subject of hoop skirts and the degree to which they exposed the damsels who wore them.

In the two Lick House Ball reviews Mark Twain jokes members of the staff and guests of the hotel, takes another dig at his old friend The Unreliable, and refers to his earlier attacks on noisy children and nosey chambermaids. In his list of distinguished guests occurs one of the few references in his works to Emperor Norton, the famous mad man, once a financier, who imagined himself the Emperor of the United States and the Protector of Mexico. His name is coupled with that of the Duke of Benicia, or "Benish" to Mark, a mythical figure as much a puff of hot air as was Benicia, the metropolis of the west, a real estate fiasco promoted by Larkin and Semple.

THE LICK HOUSE BALL

EDS. ERA: I have received a letter from the land of eternal summer—Washoe, you understand—requesting a short synopsis of the San Francisco fashions for reference. There are ten note-paper pages of it. I read it all. For two hours I worked along through it—spelling a word laboriously here and there—figuring out sentences by main strength—getting three or four of them corraled, all ragged and disjointed, and then skirmishing around after the connection—two hours of unflagging labor, determination and blasphemy, unrewarded by one solitary shadow of a suspicion of what the writer was trying to get through her head or what she could possibly be up to—until I bore down upon the three lines at the bottom of the last page, marked "P.S.," which contained the request about the fashions, and was the only paragraph in the document wherein the light of reason glimmered. All that went before it was driveling stupidity—all that the girl really wished to say was in the postscript. It was not strange that I experienced a warm fellow-feeling for the dog that drank sixty gallons of water to get at a spoonful of mush in the bottom of the tank.

The young lady signs herself "Oenone." I am not acquainted with her, but the respect, the deference which, as a white man and a Christian, I naturally feel for members of her sex, impels me to take no less pains in obliging her than were the circumstances different.

A fortunate occurrence has placed it in my power to furnish Oenone with the very latest fashions: I refer to the great ball given me at the Lick House last Thursday night by a portion of the guests of that hotel, on the occasion of my promising to "let up" on Messrs. Jerome Rice, John B. Winters, Brooks, Mason, Charley Creed, Capt. Pease, and the other "billiard sharps" of the establishment.

It was a graceful acknowledgment of my proficiency in the beautiful science of billiards, as well as of the liberality I have shown in paying for about every game I ever played in the house.

I expect I have been rather hard upon those gentlemen, but it was no fault of mine—they courted their own destruction. As one of them expressed it, they "could not resist the temptation to tackle me"; and if they baited their hooks for a sardine and caught a whale, who is to blame? Possibly it will be a comfort to Capt. Pease to know that I don't blame him, anyhow; that there is no animosity whatever, and that I feel the same filial affection, the same kindly regard, etc., etc., just as if nothing had happened.

Oenone, (or Unknown, if it is all the same to you,) the ball was a grand success. The army was present and also the navy. The nobility were represented by his Grace the Duke of Benicia, the Countess of San Jose, Lord Blessyou, Lord Geeminy, and many others whose titles and whose faces have passed from my memory. Owing to a press of imperial business, the Emperor Norton was unable to come.

The parlors were royally decorated, and the floors covered with a rich white carpet of mauve domestique, forty dollars a yard, imported from Massachusetts or the kingdom of New Jersey, I have forgotten which. The moment I entered I saw at a glance that this was the most extraordinary party ever given in San Francisco. I mentioned it to Benish, (the very friendly, not to say familiar, relations existing between myself and his Grace the Duke of Benicia, permit of my addressing him in this way without impropriety) and he said he had never seen anything like it where he came from. He said there were more diamonds here than were displayed at the very creditable effort of the Messrs. Barron, recently. This remark revived in his breast a reminiscence of that ball. He observed that the evening before it came off, he visited all the jewelry shops in town for the purpose of leasing some diamonds for his wife, who had been invited; but others had gone before him and "cleaned out" (as the facetious nobleman expressed it) every establishment. There was but one shop where a diamond remained on hand; and even there, the proprietor was obliged to tell him—though it cost him pain to do it—that he only had a quart left, and they had already been engaged by the Duchess of Goat Island, who was going to the ball and could not do without them.

The memory of the incident affected the noble Benish almost to tears, and we pursued the theme no further. After this, we relapsed into a desultory conversation in French, in which I rather had the best of him; he appeared to have an idea that he could cypher out what I was driving at, whereas I had never expected to understand him in the first place.

But you are suffering for the fashions, Oenone. I have written such things before, but only by way of burlesquing the newspaper descriptions of balls and dresses launched at the public every now and then by individuals who do not seem to know that writing fashion articles, like wet nursing, can only be done properly by women. A rightly constituted man ought to be above filching from the prerogatives of the other sex. As I have said, the fashion synopses heretofore written by myself, have been uncouth burlesques—extravagant paraphrases of the eloquence of female costume, as incomprehensible and as conflicting as Billy Birch's testimony in the case of the atrocious assassination of Erickson's bull by "Jonesy," with his infamous "stuffed club." But this time, since a lady requests it, I will choke down my distaste for such feminine employment, and write a faithful description of the queenly dresses worn at the Lick House party by several ladies whose tempers I think I can depend on. Thus:

Mrs. F. F. L. wore a superb toilette habillée of Chambry gauze; over this a charming Figaro jacket, made of mohair, or horse-hair, or something of that kind; over this again, a Raphael blouse of *cheveux de la reine*, trimmed round the bottom with lozenges formed of insertions, and around the top with bronchial troches; nothing could be more graceful than the contrast between the lozenges and the troches; over the blouse she wore a *robe de chambre* of regal magnificence, made of *Faille* silk and ornamented with macaroon (usually spelled "maccaroni") buttons set in black guipure. On the roof of her bonnet was a menagerie of rare and beautiful bugs and reptiles, and under the eaves thereof a counterfeit of the "early bird" whose specialty it hath been to work destruction upon such things since time began. To say that Mrs. L. was never more elaborately dressed in her life, would be to express an opinion within the range of possibility, at least—to say that she did or could look otherwise than charming, would be a deliberate departure from the truth.

Mrs. Wm. M. S. wore a gorgeous dress of silk bias, trimmed with tufts of ponceau feathers in the *Frondeur* style; elbowed sleeves made of chicories; plaited Swiss habit-shirt, composed of Valenciennes, *a la vielle*, embellished with a delicate nansook insertion scalloped at the edge; Lonjumeau jacket of maize-colored *Geralda*, set off with *bagnettes*, bayonets, clarinets, and one thing or other—beautiful. Rice-straw bonnet of Mechlin tulle, trimmed with devices cut out of sole-leather, representing aigrettes and arastras—or asters, whichever it is. Leather ornaments are becoming very fashionable in high society. I am told the Empress Eugenie dresses in buckskin now, altogether; so does Her Majesty the Queen of the Shoshones. It will be seen at a glance that Mrs. S's. costume upon this occasion was peculiarly suited to the serene dignity of her bearing.

Mrs. A. W. B. was arrayed in a sorrel organdy, trimmed with fustians and figaros, and canzou fichus, so disposed as to give a splendid effect without disturbing the general harmony of the dress. The body of the robe was of zero velvet, goffered, with a square pelerine of solferino *poil de chevre* amidships. The fan used by Mrs. B. was of real palm-leaf and cost four thousand dollars—the handle alone cost six bits. Her head dress was composed of a graceful cataract of white chantilly lace, surmounted by a few artificial worms, and butterflies and things, and a tasteful tarantula done in jet. It is impossible to conceive of anything more enchanting than this toilet—or the lady who wore it, either, for that matter.

Mrs. J. B. W. was dressed in a rich white satin, with a body composed of a gorgeously figured Mackinaw blanket, with five rows of ornamental brass buttons down the back. The dress was looped up at the side with several bows of No. 3 ribbon—yellow—displaying a skirt of cream-colored Valenciennes crocheted with pink crewel. The coiffure was simply a tall cone of brilliant field-flowers, upon the summit of which stood a glittering "golden beetle"—or, as we call him at home, a "straddle-bug." All who saw the beautiful Mrs. W. upon this occasion will agree that there was nothing wanting about her dress to make it attract attention in any community.

Mrs. F. was attired in an elegant Irish foulard of figured aquamarine, or aqua fortis, or something of that kind with thirty-two perpendicular rows of tulle puffings formed of black zero velvets (Fahrenheit.) Over this she wore a rich balmoral skirt—Pekin stripe—looped up at the sides with clusters of field flowers, showing the handsome dress beneath. She also wore a white Figaro postillion pea-jacket, ornamented with a profusion of Gabriel bows of crimson silk. From her head depended tasteful garlands of fresh radishes. It being natural to look charming upon all occasions, she did so upon this, of course.

Miss B. wore an elegant goffered flounce, trimmed with a grenadine of *bouillonnee*, with a crinoline waistcoat to match; pardessus open behind, embroidered with paramattas of passementerie, and further ornamented at the shoulders with epaulettes of wheat-ears and string-beans; tulle hat, embellished with blue-bells, hare-bells, hash-bells, etc., with a frontispiece formed of a single magnificent cauliflower imbedded in mashed potatoes. Thus attired Miss B. looked good enough to eat. I admit that the expression is not very refined, but when a man is hungry the similes he uses are apt to be suggested by his stomach.

It is hardly worth while to describe the costumes of the gentlemen, since, with the exception of a handsome uniform here and there (there were six naval Brigadier Generals present from the frigate *Lancaster*) they were all alike, and as usual, there was nothing worthy of particular notice in what they wore.

Oenone, I could furnish you with an accurate description of the costume of every lady who attended that party if it were safe to do it, but it isn't, you know. Over in Washoe I generally say what I please about anybody and everybody, because my obliging fellow citizens have learned to put up with it; but here, common prudence teaches me to speak of those only who are slow to anger, when writing about ladies. I had rather lose my scalp, anyhow, than wound a lady's feelings.

But there is one thing you can rest assured of, Oenone: The pleasantest parties in the world are those given at the Lick House every now and then, and to which scarcely any save the guests of the establishment are invited; and the ladies are handsomer, and dress with more taste and greater magnificence—but there come the children again.—When that last invoice of fifteen hundred infants come around and get to romping about my door with the others, and hurrahing for their several favorite candidates for Governor (unaware that the election is over, poor little miscreants,) I cannot write with such serene comfort as I do when they are asleep. Yet there is nothing I love so dearly as a clean, fat, healthy infant. I calculate to eat that whole tribe before I leave the Lick House.

Now, do you know, Oenone—however, I hear the stately tread of that inveterate chambermaid. She always finds this room in a state of chaos, and she always leaves it as trim as a parlor. But her instincts infallibly impel her to march in here just when I feel least like marching out. I do not know that I have ever begged permission to write "only a few moments longer"—never with my tongue, at any rate, although I may have *looked* it with my expressive glass eye. But she cares nothing for such spooney prayers. She is a soldier in the army of the household; she knows her duty, and she allows nothing to interfere with its rigid performance. She reminds me of U. S. Grant; she marches in her grand military way to the centre of the room, and comes to an "order arms" with her broom and her slop-bucket; then she bends on me a look of uncompromising determination, and I reluctantly haul down my flag. I abandon my position—I evacuate the premises—I retire in good order —I vamose the ranch. Because that look of hers says in plain, crisp language, "I don't want you here. If you are not gone in two minutes, I propose to move upon your works!" But I bear the chambermaid no animosity.

FROM THE *Golden Era*, SEPT. 27, 1863.

ALL ABOUT THE FASHIONS

SAN FRANCISCO, June 19.

EDS. ENTERPRISE:—I have just received, per Wells-Fargo, the following sweet scented little note, written in a microscopic hand in the centre of a delicate sheet of paper—like a wedding invitation or a funeral notice —and I feel it my duty to answer it.

"VIRGINIA, June 16.

"MR. MARK TWAIN:—*Do* tell us something about the fashions. I am dying to know what the ladies of San Francisco are wearing. Do, now, tell us all you know about it, won't you? Pray, excuse brevity, for I am in *such* a hurry. BETTIE.

"P. S.—Please burn this as soon as you have read it."

"*Do* tell us"—and she is in "*such* a hurry." Well, I never knew a girl in my life who could write three consecutive sentences without italicizing a word. They can't do it, you know. Now, if I had a wife, and she—however, I don't think I shall have one this week, and it is hardly worth while to borrow trouble.

Bettie, my love, you do me proud. In thus requesting me to fix up the fashions for you in an intelligent manner, you pay a compliment to my critical and observant eye and my varied and extensive information, which a mind less perfectly balanced than mine could scarcely contemplate without excess of vanity. Will I tell you something about the fashions? I will, Bettie—you better bet you bet, Betsey, my darling. I learned these expressions from the Unreliable; like all the phrases which fall from his lips, they are frightfully vulgar—but then they sound rather musical than otherwise.

A happy circumstance has put it in my power to furnish you the fashions from headquarters—as it were, Bettie: I refer to the assemblage of fashion, elegance and loveliness called together in the parlor of the Lick House last night—[a party given by the proprietors on the occasion of my paying up that little balance due on my board bill.] I will give a brief and lucid description of the dresses worn by several of the ladies of my acquaintance who were present.

Mrs. B. was arrayed in a superb speckled foulard, with the stripes running fore and aft, and with collets and camails to match; also, a rotonde of Chantilly lace, embroidered with blue and yellow dogs, and birds and things, done in crewel, and edged with a Solferino fringe four inches deep—lovely. Mrs. B. is tall, and graceful and beautiful, and the general effect of her costume was to render her appearance extremely lively.

Miss J. W. wore a charming robe polonais of scarlet ruche *a la vielle*, with yellow fluted flounces of rich bombazine, fourteen inches wide; low neck and short sleeves; also a Figaro vest of bleached domestic—selvedge edge turned down with a back stitch, and trimmed with festoons of blue chicory taffetas—gay?—I reckon not. Her head-dress was the sweetest thing you ever saw: a bunch of stately ostrich plumes—red and white—springing like fountains above each ear, with a crown between, consisting of a single *fleur de soleil*, fresh from garden—Ah, me! Miss W. looked enchantingly pretty; however, there was nothing unusual about that—I have seen her look so, even in a milder costume.

Mrs. J. B. W. wore a heavy rat-colored brocade silk, studded with large silver stars, and trimmed with organdie; balloon sleeves of nankeen pique, gathered at the wrist, cut bias and hollowed out some at the elbow; also a burnous of black Honiton lace, scalloped, and embroidered in violent colors with a battle piece representing the taking of Holland by the Dutch; low neck, and high-heeled shoes; gloves; palm-leaf fan; hoops; her head-dress consisting of a simple maroon colored Sontag, with festoons of blue illusion depending from it; upon her bosom reposed a gorgeous bouquet of real sage brush imported from Washoe. Mrs. W. looked regally handsome. If every article of dress worn by her on this occasion had been multiplied seven times, I do not believe it would have improved her appearance any.

Miss C. wore an elegant *Cheveux de la Reine* (with ruffles and furbelows trimmed with bands of guipure round the bottom), and a mohair Garibaldi shirt; her unique head-dress, was crowned with a graceful *pomme de terre* (Limerick French) and she had her hair done up in papers—greenbacks. The effect was very rich, partly owing to the market value of the material, and partly to the general loveliness of the lady herself.

Miss A. H. wore a splendid Lucia de Lammermoor, trimmed with green baize; also, a cream-colored mantilla-shaped *pardessus*, with a deep gore in the neck, and embellished with a wide greque of taffeta ribbon, and otherwise garnished with ruches, and radishes and things. Her *coiffure* was a simple wreath of sardines on a string. She was lovely to a fault.

Now, what do you think of that effort, Bettie (I wish I knew your other name) for an unsanctified newspaper reporter devoid of a milliner's education? Doesn't it strike you that there are more brains and fewer oysters in my head than a casual acquaintance with me would lead one to suppose? Ah, well—what I don't know Bet, is hardly worth the finding out, I can tell you. I could have described the dresses of all the ladies in that party, but I was afraid to meddle with those of strangers, because I might unwittingly get something wrong, and give offense. You see strangers never exercise any charity in matters of this kind—they always get mad at the least inaccuracies of description concerning their apparel, and make themselves disagreeable. But if you will just rig yourself up according to the modes I have furnished you, Bet, you'll do, you know—you can weather the circus.

You will naturally wish to be informed as to the most fashionable style of male attire, and I may as well give you an idea of my own personal appearance at the party. I wore one of Mr. Lawlor's shirts, and Mr. Ridgway's vest, and Dr. Wayman's coat, and Mr. Camp's hat, and Mr. Paxton's boots, and Jerry Long's white kids, and Judge Gilchrist's cravat, and the Unreliable's brass seal-ring, and Dr. Toll-road Mc-

Donald's pantaloons—and if you have an idea that they are anyways short in the legs, do you just climb into them once, sweetness. The balance of my outfit I gathered up indiscriminately from various individuals whose names I have forgotten and have now no means of ascertaining, as I thoughtlessly erased the marks from the different garments this morning. But I looked salubrious, B., if ever a man did.

Messrs Editors, I never wrote such a personal article as this before. I expect I had better go home, now. Well, I have been here long enough, anyhow. I didn't come down to stay always, in the first place. I don't know of anything more here that I want to see. I might just as well go home now as not. I have been wanting to go home for a good while. I don't see why I haven't gone before this. They all say it is healthier up there than it is here. I believe it. I have not been very well for a week. I don't eat enough, I expect. But I would stay here just as long as I pleased though, if I wanted to. But I don't. Well, I don't care—I am going home—that is the amount of it — and very soon, too — maybe sooner.

FROM THE *Golden Era*, SEPT. 27, 1863

THE PIONEERS' BALL

IT WAS ESTIMATED that four hundred persons were present at the ball. The gentlemen wore the orthodox costume for such occasions, and the ladies were dressed the best they knew how. N. B.—Most of these ladies were pretty, and some of them absolutely beautiful. Four out of every five ladies present were pretty. The ratio at the Colfax party was two out of every five. I always keep the run of these things. While upon this department of the subject, I may as well tarry a moment and furnish you with descriptions of some of the most noticeable costumes.

Mrs. W. M. was attired in an elegant *pate de foi gras*, made expressly for her, and was greatly admired.

Miss S. had her hair done up. She was the centre of attraction for the gentlemen, and the envy of all the ladies.

Miss G. W. was tastefully dressed in a *tout ensemble,* and was greeted with deafening applause wherever she went.

Mrs. C. N. was superbly arrayed in white kid gloves. Her modest and engaging manner accorded well with the unpretending simplicity of her costume, and caused her to be regarded with absorbing interest by every one.

The charming Miss M. M. B. appeared in a thrilling waterfall, whose exceeding grace and volume compelled the homage of pioneers and emigrants alike. How beautiful she was!

The queenly Mrs. L. B. was attractively attired in her new and beautiful false teeth, and the *bon jour* effect they naturally produced was heightened by her enchanting and well-sustained smile. The manner of this lady is charmingly pensive and melancholy, and her troops of admirers desired no greater happiness than to get on the scent of her sozodont-sweetened sighs and track her through her sinuous course among the gay and restless multitude.

Miss R. P., with that repugnance to ostentation in dress which is so peculiar to her, was attired in a simple white lace collar, fastened with a neat pearl-button solitaire. The fine contrast between the sparkling vivacity of her natural optic and the steadfast attentiveness of her placid glass eye was the subject of general and enthusiastic remark.

The radiant and sylph-like Mrs. T., late of your state, wore hoops. She showed to good advantage, and created a sensation wherever she appeared. She was the gayest of the gay.

Miss C. L. B. had her fine nose elegantly enameled, and the easy grace with which she blew it from time to time, marked her as a cultivated and accomplished woman of the world; its exquisitely modulated tone excited the admiration of all who had the happiness to hear it.

Being offended with Miss X., and our acquaintance having ceased prematurely, I will take this opportunity of observing to her that it is of no use for her to be slopping off to every ball that takes place, and flourishing around with a brass oyster-knife skewered through her waterfall, and smiling her sickly smile through her decayed teeth, with her dismal pug nose in the air. There is no use in it—she don't fool anybody. Everybody knows that she is old; everybody knows she is repaired (you might almost say built) with artificial bones and hair and muscles and things, from the ground up — put together scrap by scrap — and everybody knows, also, that all one would have to do would be to pull out her key-pin and she would go to pieces like a Chinese puzzle. There, now, my faded flower, take that paragraph home with you and amuse yourself with it; and if ever you turn your wart of a nose up at me again I will sit down and write something that will just make you rise up and howl.

FROM THE *Golden Era*, NOV. 26, 1865. [T. E.]

FASHIONS

I ONCE MADE UP MY MIND to keep the ladies of the State of Nevada posted upon the fashions, but I found it hard to do. The fashions got so shaky that it was hard to tell what was good orthodox fashion, and what heretical and vulgar. This shakiness still obtains in everything pertaining to a lady's dress except her bonnet and her shoes. Some wear waterfalls, some wear nets, some wear cataracts of curls, and a few go bald, among the old maids; so no man can swear to any particular "fashion" in the matter of hair.

The same uncertainty seems to prevail regarding hoops. Little "highflyer" schoolgirls of bad associations, and a good many women of full growth, wear no hoops at all. And we suspect these, as quickly and as naturally as we suspect a woman who keeps a poodle. Some who I know to be ladies, wear the ordinary moderate-sized hoop, and some who I also know to be ladies, wear the new hoop of the "spread-eagle" pattern—and some wear the latter who are not elegant and virtuous ladies—but that is a thing that may be said of any fashion whatever, of course.

The new hoops with a spreading base look only tolerably well. They are not bell-shaped—the "spread" is much more abrupt than that. It is tent-shaped; I do not mean an army tent, but a circus tent—which comes down steep and small half way and then shoots suddenly out horizontally and spreads abroad. To critically examine these hoops—to get the best effect—one should stand on the corner of Montgomery and look up a steep street like Clay or Washington. As the ladies loop their dresses up till they lie in folds and festoons on the spreading hoop, the effect presented by a furtive glance up a steep street is very charming. It reminds me of how I used to peep under circus tents when I was a boy and see a lot of mysterious legs tripping about with no visible bodies attached to them. And what handsome vari-colored, gold-clasped garters they wear now-a-days! But for the new spreading hoops, I might have gone on thinking ladies still tied up their stockings with common strings and ribbons as they used to do when I was a boy and they presumed upon my youth to indulge in little freedoms in the way of arranging their apparel which they do not dare to venture upon in my presence now.

FROM THE *Golden Era*, FEB. 25, 1866.

II. STAR REPORTER IN VIRGINIA CITY

Mark Twain

AND DAN DE QUILLE

IT WILL BE REMEMBERED that Samuel Clemens joined the staff of the Virginia City Territorial Enterprise in 1862 to sub for Dan de Quille, legal name William Wright, while the latter was taking a year's vacation in the States. By the time Dan de Quille returned in the fall of '63, Mark Twain was indispensable, and Joe Goodman decided to keep both humorists—perhaps so that they could work out on each other when short of other subjects. Hardly had Mark Twain left Virginia City on his vacation trip to the coast before Dan remarked that "the moral tone of this column will be much improved" through its former writer's absence. That was the first shot in a literary feud that kept Washoe and California laughing throughout the winter. The mock-battle between Dan de Quille and Mark Twain proved to be even funnier than had been the one between Mark Twain and the Unreliable the previous winter, or the long-standing one between Daggett and Goodman for title of chief poet of the camp. And the more the two humorists bantered each other in public, the closer friends they became in private.

Perhaps in order to keep an eye on each other, they got rooms together on the second floor of a brick building on B street. They made excellent roommates, for they both liked to smoke in bed and both were always ready to get up for a midnight snack of oysters. Across the hall lived Tom Fitch, editor of the rival paper, and his wife, who often made pies for her bachelor friends. Soon rumor had it that Mark Twain not only stole pies from Mrs. Fitch but was guilty of murdering her troublesome cat by hanging it out the window. Also some of the boys whispered that Mark Twain helped himself freely to the Fitch woodbox, which stood in the hall. Dan de Quille, in the first article of this series, does his best to disprove this foul charge while his friend is down in Carson City reporting the Constitutional Convention. It is interesting to note how similar were the tones and methods of the two humorists. They both spoke the language of the frontier.

Stories that a rumpus raised by Mark Twain's "Empire City Massacre Hoax" had dimmed the Washoe Giant's taste for blood and gore are amply refuted in his account of poor Dan's injuries from falling off his noble steed. When Dan's saddle-girth broke, throwing him from his horse and giving him a twisted knee, Mark published an account of "the frightful accident" which Dan always insisted made his mother swoon when she read it, back in Missouri. To make up for his unkind article, Mark brought home to the invalid an orange and a cigar—the orange selected for its coolness and the cigar for its soothing effects. Shortly thereafter, Dan had an opportunity to get even when Mark Twain put on gloves with an English boxer at M. Chauvel's gymnasium, where all of the members of the Enterprise staff took fencing lessons. Mark Twain was fooling with Dawson, but Dawson forgot to fool with Mark Twain. The nose mangling that resulted kept Mark Twain from work for several days and gave Dan de Quille all the scope in the world for his fun. Tradition has it that Mark Twain finally took his nose into seclusion at Silver Mountain, Alpine County, California, only to discover that Dan's accounts of the marvel had preceded him. Three cheers were given as the nose was seen coming out of the stage, and an old dame, when allowed to touch it, declared that she had experienced the happiest moment of her life.

HOUSE-KEEPING WITH MARK TWAIN

BY DAN DE QUILLE

WE (MARK AND I) have the "sweetest" little parlor and the snuggest little bedroom (and its only three floors from the ground) all to ourselves. Here we come every night and live—breathe, move and have our being, also our toddies. As Mark has already hinted to the world in his modest way, through the columns of the *Territorial Enterprise*, that "our furniture alone cost $28,000, in Europe," I need only add that our upholstery, etc., cost $15,000 more, in—a horn. We have a very good dodge for getting wood, we leave our door open when we go out (we have nothing in our rooms but is so fearfully and wonderfully made, and of such valuable materials, that we have no fear of thieves—why, a thief would run from them at first sight! he would feel, just to gaze on them, as though a rope were already about his neck) so we leave our door open when we go out, and the fellows that are hired to carry up wood to the rooms, make a mistake nearly every day and pile a lot in our parlor. I never have seen the fellow making these mistakes, but Mark assures me that the wood all gets into our parlor that way. I suppose he was right—it looks very plausible, but lately I've been thinking that it was rather strange that the fellow quit making these mistakes the very day that Mark went down to Carson to report the proceedings of the Constitutional Convention, and hasn't made a single mistake since. Now it would be a most singular coincidence if the fellow should commence piling wood into our parlor again the very night Mark returns. I think I shall remember to observe if anything of the kind occurs; it would really be *remarkable* if his presence should so confuse the poor man.

I used to feel quite uneasy in mind at times while these awkward mistakes about rooms were occuring, as the neighbors used to nearly always branch out about the enormity of the sin of wood-stealing when Mark or I came about. Mark said there was no use in listening to what they were saying as he could prove by history that in all ages there were found wicked persons who took a sort of fiendish delight in persecuting the modest, the virtuous and the innocent; then he cited the case of our Saviour who was crucified by wicked men, "and," said he, "I think there are those who, being envious of our great reputation for virtue and honesty, are laying plans to injure us in the eyes of the world. But, Dan'l," said he, "we can live them down—yes, live them down!" "Do you know," said he, whispering in my ear, "that I sometimes think our enemies *bring this wood into our room!*" and he looked with a look so unfathomably deep, so sagacious and wise, just as he turned to walk off, that I could not help admiring him.

That night, when we reached home, near midnight, a bigger lot than ever of wood was found in our room. Poor Mark saw it, and clapping his hands to his forehead heaved a great sigh and pointing to the goodly heap of billets, said—"Behold the work of the persecutors!" then staggered to a seat. I supposed he had fainted and was about to sieze the water-pitcher and pour its contents over his head, when, seeing the movement, with a wave of his hand, he said, "Never mind, 'twas but a passing throe of agony wrung from my iron soul by the persistency of our secret foes!—slap in a few sticks of that nice nut-pine and make up a jolly fire; methinks a toddy, piping hot, would rid this breast of the woes planted there by our skulking enemies!"

This second view of the case may possibly have been the correct one—instead of the wood having been placed in our room through the mistake of a low-born hireling, it may have been cunningly insinuated into our apartment by an enemy to work out upon us some hellish plot against our purity of character. As the persecution ceased the very day my friend and partner left, I cannot but feel that these persecutions—if such they really were—were aimed particularly against my poor guileless Mark. If there should be a recurrence of these singular proceedings on his return, I shall feel very uneasy for him.

The above is about all that has occurred to mar our peace since we began housekeeping—to be sure, soap, candles, towels, etc., have been mysteriously left in our rooms, but these are minor troubles and give us little uneasiness.

FROM THE *Golden Era*, DEC. 6, 1863

MARK TWAIN AND DAN DE QUILLE HORS DE COMBAT

Recent issues of the *Territorial Enterprise* give the particulars of a series of terrible calamities that have befallen two of the literary celebrities of Silver Land:

FRIGHTFUL ACCIDENT TO DAN DE QUILLE

OUR TIME-HONORED CONFRERE, Dan, met with a disastrous accident, Tuesday, while returning from American City on a vicious Spanish horse, the result of which accident is that at the present writing he is confined to his bed and suffering great bodily pain.

He was coming down the road at the rate of a hundred miles an hour, (as stated in his will, which he made shortly after the accident) and on turning a sharp corner, he suddenly hove in sight of a horse standing square across the channel; he signaled for the starboard, and put his helm down instantly, but too late, after all; he was swinging to port, and before he could straighten down, he swept like an avalanche against the transom of the strange craft; his larboard knee coming in contact with the rudder-post of the adversary. Dan was wrenched from his saddle and thrown some three hundred yards (according to his own statement, made in his will above mentioned) alighting upon solid ground, and bursting himself open from the chin to the pit of the stomach; his head was also caved in out of sight, and his hat was afterward extracted in a bloody and damaged condition from between his lungs; he must have bounced end-for-end after he struck first, because it is evident he received a concussion from the rear that broke his heart; one leg was jammed up in his body nearly to his throat, and the other was so torn and mutilated that it pulled out when they attempted to lift him into the hearse which we had sent to the scene of the disaster, under the general impression that he might need it; both arms were indiscriminately broken up until they were jointed like a bamboo; his back was considerably fractured and bent into the shape of a rail fence.

Aside from these injuries, however, he sustained no other damage. They brought some of him home in the hearse, and the balance on a dray. His first remark showed that the powers of his great mind had not been impaired by the accident, nor his profound judgment destroyed—he said he wouldn't have cared a d—n—if it had been anybody but himself. He then made his will, after which he set to work with that earnestness and singleness of purpose which have always distinguished him, to abuse the assemblage of anxious hash-proprietors who had called on business, and to repudiate their bills with his customary promptness and impartiality.

Dan may have exaggerated the above details in some respects, but he charged us to report them thus, and it is a source of genuine pleasure to us to have the opportunity of doing it. Our noble old friend is recoving fast, and what is left of him will be around the breweries again today, just as usual.

AN INFAMOUS PROCEEDING

Some three days since, in returning to this city from American Flat, we had the misfortune to be thrown from a fiery untamed steed of

Spanish extraction—a very strong extract, too. Our knee was sprained by our fall and we were for a day or two confined to our room—of course knowing little of what was going on in the great world outside. Mark Twain, our confrere and room-mate, a man in whom we trusted, was our only visitor during our seclusion. We saw some actions of his that almost caused us to suspect him of contemplating treachery towards us, but it was not until we regained in some degree the use of our maimed limb that we discovered the full extent—the infamousness of this wretch's treasonable and inhuman plottings. He wrote such an account of our accident as would lead the public to believe that we were injured beyond all hope of recovery. The next day he tied a small piece of second-hand crape about his hat, and putting on a lugubrious look, went to the Probate Court, and getting down on his knees commenced praying—it was the first time he ever prayed for anything or to anybody—for letters of administration on our estate. Before going to the Court to pray he had stuffed the principal part of our estate—consisting of numerous shares in the Pewterinctum—into his vest pocket; also had secured our tooth-brush and had been using it a whole day. He had on our only clean shirt and best socks, also was sporting our cane and smoking our meerschaum. But what most showed his heartlessness and utter depravity was the disposition he made of our boots and coat. When we missed these we applied to Marshall Cooke. The Marshall said he thought he could find them for us. He went on to say that for sometime past he had noticed the existence of a suspicious intimacy between Twain and a nigger saloon keeper, who had a dead-fall on North B street. Proceeding to this palace he found that he was correct in his conjecture. Twain had taken our boots and coat to the darkey, and traded them off for a bottle of vile whiskey, with which he got drunk; and when the police were about to snatch him for drunkenness, he commenced blubbering, saying that he was "overcome for the untimely death of poor Dan." By this dodge he escaped the lock-up, but if he does not shortly give up our Pewterinctum stock—which is of fabulous value—shell out our tooth-brush and take off our socks and best shirt, he will not so easily escape the Territorial Prison.

P. S.—We have just learned that he stole the crape he tied about his hat from the door knob of Three's engine house, South B street.

MARK TWAIN TAKES A LESSON IN THE MANLY ART

We may have said some harsh things of Mark Twain, but now we take them all back. We feel like weeping for him—yea, we would fall on his breast and mingle our tears with his'n. But those manly shirt front of his air now a bloody one, and his nose is swollen to such an extent that to fall on his breast would be an utter impossibility.

Yesterday, he brought back all our things and promised us that he intended hereafter to lead a virtuous life. This was in the forenoon; in the afternoon he commenced the career of virtue he had marked out for himself and took a first lesson in boxing. Once he had the big gloves on, he imagined that he weighed a ton and could whip his weight in Greek-fire. He waded into a professor of the "manly art" like one of Howlan's rotary batteries, and the professor, in a playful way he has, when he wants to take the conceit out of forward pupils, let one fly straight out from the shoulder and "busted" Mr. Twain in the "snoot," sending him reeling—not exactly to grass, but across a bench—with two bountiful streams of "claret" spouting from his nostrils. At first his nose was smashed out till it covered nearly the whole of his face and looked like a large piece of tripe, but it was finally scraped into some resemblance of a nose, when he rushed away for surgical advice. Pools of gore covered the floor of the Club Room where he fought, and he left a bloody trail for half a mile through the city. It is estimated that he lost several hogsheads of blood in all. He procured a lot of sugar of lead and other cooling lotions and spent the balance of the day in applying them with towels and sponges.

After dark, he ventured forth with his nose swollen to the size of several junk bottles—a vast, inflammed and pulpy old snoot—to get advice about having it amputated. None of his friends recognize him now, and he spends his time in solitude, contemplating his ponderous vermillion smeller in a two-bit mirror, which he bought for that purpose. We cannot comfort him, for we know his nose will never be a nose again. It always was somewhat lopsided; now it is a perfect lump of blubber. Since the above was in type, the doctors have decided to amputate poor Mark Twain's smeller. A new one is to be made for him of a quarter of veal.

FROM THE *Golden Era,* MAY 1, 1864 [T.E.]

On

WASHOE LOCALS

DURING MARK TWAIN'S *last winter in Virginia City the* Golden Era *occasionally reprinted a paragraph or even a full article from his writing for the* Territorial Enterprise. *His reputation was growing. His interests were widening, as these five short sketches show.*

Bigler vs Tahoe *is the first record of Mark Twain's objection to the name "Tahoe," which he later maintained in* Innocents Abroad *was Piute for "grasshopper soup." He apparently objected to the name on ethnological rather than political grounds; he didn't like the "Digger Indians" or anything concerned with them. Ross Browne agreed with him, claiming that "Tahoe," if it meant anything in Indian, meant whiskey. Mark Twain's favorite lake had been variously christened "Mountain Lake," "Lake Boupland," and "Lake de Groot" before it was officially named Bigler after the governor in office at the time it was surveyed. When the Republicans gained control of state politics, some one asked what Bigler had done to have a lake named after him, and the San Francisco* Bulletin *proposed and popularized the Indian word "Tahoe." Today the lake is always called "Tahoe," although its official name remains "Bigler."*

In Virginia City, heart of Storey County, Mark Twain, the moralist, had cause to complain of the lax treatment of murderers. "Bad men" flourished on the Comstock, the territorial judges headed by Judge Turner were notoriously corrupt, and men like Langford Peel used their guns without fear of punishment from the law. In his tirade against lawlessness, Mark Twain could not resist mentioning Cain's murder of Abel, a crime which so interested him that he once proposed dedicating a book to Cain.

The greeting to Artemus Ward was written while that genial showman was taking San Francisco by storm. Advertised to speak on "Brigham Young's Mother-in-Law; Showing how Many there are of Her," he delivered droll nonsense under the title of "Babes of the Wood."

Before becoming a highly successful lecturer, Ward had made his reputation as a journalist, posing as an exhibitor of wax works who wrote misspelled letters on national affairs to the Cleveland Plain Dealer. Mark Twain, in welcoming him to Virginia City, imitated the methods of Ward's famous letters. In the blurb he referred to two of his own local hits—to the large feet he had attributed to City Marshall Perry and to "Missus Hopkins' skulp," gory relic of the "Dutch Nick Massacre." Artemus Ward's hilarious visit to Virginia City stimulated Clemens to try a larger market for his work and suggested to him the idea of lecturing. Fortunately his welcome to Ward is the only instance of his succumbing to Ward's spelling, a vice which broke out like a rash among the coast humorists, even counting Dan de Quille as a temporary victim.

Though the full effect of Mark Twain's burlesque of Frederick Halm's famous melodrama, "Ingomar, the Barbarian," could be obtained only through the painful course of reading that musty play, a good deal of the fun is self-explanatory. The barbarian inhabitants of Washoe enjoyed seeing the Gothic barbarian Ingomar win the cultivated Greek maiden Parthenia with the aid of native roughness and the lyric containing the famous line: "Two souls with but a single thought, two hearts that beat as one." The play was also the object of Harte's satire in "A Night at Wingdam." Readers of Ingomar should recognize Silver City and American Flat as suburbs of Virginia City, should remember that this was the time of the Reese River gold rush, and should appreciate the digs at the local redskins.

The pretended answer to a correspondent, "Information Wanted," retains much of its original interest, gives a fair sketch of Nevada history, and introduces Mark Twain's favorite character, John Smith. (He dedicated his first book to the Smiths, hoping they would all buy copies.) Mark Twain's description of Washoe is interestingly supplemented by Goodman's poem on Virginia City, one stanza of which read:

"In youth when I did love, did love
  "(To quote the sexton's homely ditty),
"I lived six thousand feet above
  "Sea-level, in Virginia City.
"The site was bleak, the houses small
  "The narrow streets unpaved and slanting,
"But now it seems to me of all
  "The spots on earth the most entrancing."

BIGLER vs. TAHOE

[*In the* TERRITORIAL ENTERPRISE *appears a "Letter from Lake Bigler," signed "Grub" and addressed personally to "Mr. Twain"—and that rough and ready writer last named, who does the humorous local columns of the aforesaid journal, discourses his friend "Grub," thus wise:*]

HOPE SOME EARLY BIRD will catch this Grub the next time he calls Lake Bigler by so disgustingly sick and silly a name as "Lake Tahoe." I have removed the offensive word from his letter and substituted the old one, which at least has a Christian English twang about it whether it is pretty or not. Of course Indian names are more fitting than any others for our beautiful lakes and rivers, which knew their race ages ago, perhaps in the morning of creation, but let us have none so repulsive to the ear as "Tahoe" for the beautiful relic of fairyland forgotten and left asleep in the snowy Sierras when the little elves fled from their ancient haunts and quitted the earth. They say it means "Fallen Leaf"—well suppose it meant fallen devil or fallen angel, would that render its hideous, discordant syllables more endurable? Not if I know myself. I yearn for the scalp of the soft-shell crab—be he Indian or white man—who conceived of that spoony, slobbering, summer-complaint of a name. Why, if I had a grudge against a half-price nigger, I wouldn't be mean enough to call him by such an epithet as that; then, how am I to hear it applied to the enchanted mirror that the viewless spirits of the air make their toilets by, and hold my peace? "Tahoe"—it sounds as weak as soup for a sick infant. "Tahoe" be—forgotten! I just saved my reputation that time. In conclusion, "Grub," I mean to start to Lake Bigler myself, Monday morning, or somebody shall come to grief.

FROM THE *Golden Era*, SEPT. 13, 1863. [T. E.]

ON MURDERS

WE AVERAGE ABOUT four murders in the first degree a month, in Virginia, but we never convict anybody. The murder of Abel, by his brother Cain, would rank as an eminently justifiable homicide up there in Storey county. When a man merely attempts to kill another, there, and fails in his object, our Police Judge handles him with pitiless severity. He has him instantly arrested, gives him some good advice, and requests him to leave the country. This has been found to have a very salutary effect. The criminal goes home and thinks the matter over profoundly, and concludes to stay with us. But he feels badly—he feels very badly, for days and days together.

FROM THE *Golden Era,* NOV. 22, 1863.
REPRINTED FROM THE S. F. *Morning Call.*

GREETING TO ARTEMUS WARD

WE UNDERSTAND THAT Artemus Ward contemplates visiting this region to deliver his lectures, and perhaps make some additions to his big "sho." In his last letter to us he appeared particularly anxious to 'sekure' a kupple ov horned todes; alsowe, a lizard which it may be persessed of 2 tales, or any komical snaix, an enny sich little unconsidered trifles, as the poets say, which they do not interest the kommun mind. Further, be it nown, that I would like a opportunity for to maik a moddel in wax of a average size wash-owe man, with feet attached, as an kompanion pictur to a waxen figger of a nigger I hev sekured, at an large outlaye, whitch it has a unnatural big hed onto it. Could you alsowe manage to gobbel up the skulp of the layte Missus Hopkins? I adore sich foot-prints of atrocity as it were, muchly. I was roominatin on gittin a bust of mark Twain, but I've kwit kontemplatin the work. They tell me down heer too the Ba that the busts air so kommon it wood ony bee an waist of wax too git un kounterfit presentiment."

We shall assist Mr. Ward in every possible way about making his Washoe collection and have no doubt but he will pick up many curious things during his sojourn.

FROM THE *Golden Era,* NOV. 29, 1863. [T. E.]

"INGOMAR" OVER THE MOUNTAINS

[During the Fall Season of Mr. Maguire's Dramatic troupe at his new Opera House in Virginia City, the TERRITORIAL ENTERPRISE *has indulged its readers with an extraordinary succession of humorous, pungent and peculiar critiques. The player-folk presented "Ingomar, the Barbarian," and Mark Twain did the piece after this funny fashion:]*

ACT. 1.—Mrs. Claughley appears in the costume of a healthy Greek matron (from Limerick). She urges Parthenia, her daughter, to marry Polydor, and save her father from being sold out by the sheriff—the old man being in debt for assessments.

Scene 2.—Polydor—who is a wealthy, spindle-shanked, stingy old stockbroker—prefers his suit and is refused by the Greek maiden—by the accomplished Greek maiden, we may say, since she speaks English without any perceptible foreign accent.

Scene 3.—The Comanches capture Parthenia's father, old Myron (who is the chief and only blacksmith in his native village) they tear him from his humble cot, and carry him away, to Reese River. They hold him as a slave. It will cost thirty ounces of silver to get him out of soak.

Scene 4.—Dusty times in the Myron family. Their house is mortgaged—they are without dividends—they cannot "stand the raise."

Parthenia, in this extremity, applies to Polydor. He sneeringly advises her to shove out after her exiled parent herself.

She shoves!

ACT II.—Camp of the Comanches. In the foreground, several of the tribe throwing dice for tickets in Wright's Gift Entertainment. In the background, old Myron packing faggots on a jack. The weary slave weeps—he sighs—he slobbers. Grief lays her heavy hand upon him.

Scene 2.—Comanches on the war-path, headed by the chief, Ingomar. Parthenia arrives and offers to remain as a hostage while old Myron returns home and borrows thirty dollars to pay his ransom with. It was pleasant to note the varieties of dress displayed in the costumes of Ingomar and his comrades. It was also pleasant to observe that in those ancient times the better class of citizens were able to dress in ornamental carriage robes, and even the rank and file indulged in Benkert boots, albeit some of the latter appeared not to have been blacked for several days.

Scene 3.—Parthenia and Ingomar alone in the woods. "Two souls with but a single thought, etc." She tells him that is love. He "can't see it."

Scene 4.—The thing works around about as we expected it would in the first place. Ingomar gets stuck after Parthenia.

Scene 5.—Ingomar declares his love—he attempts to embrace her—she waves him off, gently, but firmly—she remarks, "Not too brash, Ing., not too brash, now!" Ingomar subsides. They finally flee away, and hie them to Parthenia's home.

ACTS III and IV.—Joy! Joy! From the summit of a hill, Parthenia beholds once more the spires and domes of Silver City.

Scene 2.—Silver City. Enter Myron. Tableau! Myron begs for an extension on his note—he has not yet raised the whole ransom, but he is ready to pay two dollars and a half on account.

Scene 3.—Myron tells Ingomar he must shuck himself, and dress like a Christian; he must shave; he must work; he must give up his sword! His rebellious spirit rises. Behold Parthenia tames it with the mightier spirit of Love. Ingomar weakens—he lets down—he is utterly demoralized.

Scene 4.—Enter old Timarch, Chief of Police. He offers Ingomar—but this scene is too noble to be trifled with in burlesque.

Scene 5.—Polydor presents his bill—213 drachmas. Busted again—the old man cannot pay. Ingomar compromises by becoming the slave of Polydor.

Scene 6.—The Comanches again, with Thorne at their head! He asks who enslaved the chief? Ingomar points to Polydor. Lo! Thorne seizes the trembling broker, and snatches him bald-headed!

Scene 7.—Enter the Chief of Police again. He makes a treaty with the Comanches. He gives them a ranch apiece. He decrees that they shall build a town on the American Flat, and appoints great Ingomar to be its Mayor! [Applause by the supes.]

Scene 8.—Grand tableau—Comanches, police, Pi-Utes, and citizens generally—Ingomar and Parthenia hanging together in the centre. The old thing—The old poetical quotation, we mean—They double on it—Ingomar observing "Two souls with but a single Thought," and she slinging in the other line, "Two Hearts that Beat as one." Thus united at last in a fond embrace, they sweetly smiled upon the orchestra and the curtain fell.

FROM THE *Golden Era*, NOV. 29, 1863. [T.E.]

WASHOE

INFORMATION WANTED

[A citizen of Virginia, Washoe's world-famed metropolis, lately received a letter from a friend in Missouri who "Wanted Information" con-

cerning Silver-Land. This letter was handed over to Mark Twain. In the TERRITORIAL ENTERPRISE *we find the whole correspondence:*]

SPRINGFIELD, MO., April 12.

DEAR SIR:—My object in writing to you is to have you give me a full history of Nevada: What is the character of its climate? What are the productions of the earth? Is it healthy? What diseases do they die of mostly? Do you think it would be advisable for a man who can make a living in Missouri to emigrate to that part of the country? There are several of us who would emigrate there in the spring if we could ascertain to a certainty that it is a much better country than this. I suppose you know Joel H. Smith? He used to live here; he lives in Nevada now; they say he owns considerable in a mine there. Hoping to hear from you soon, etc., I remain yours, truly, WILLIAM ——.

DEAREST WILLIAM:—Pardon my familiarity—but that name touchingly reminds me of the loved and lost, whose name was similar. I have taken the contract to answer your letter, and although we are now strangers, I feel we shall cease to be so if we ever become acquainted with each other. The thought is worthy of attention, William. I will now respond to your several propositions in the order in which you have fulminated them.

Your object in writing is to have me give you a full history of Nevada. The flattering confidence you repose in me, William, is only equalled by the modesty of your request. I could detail the history of Nevada in five hundred pages octavo, but as you have never done me any harm, I will spare you, though it will be apparent to everybody that I would be justified in taking advantage of you if I were a mind to do it.

However, I will condense. Nevada was discovered many years ago by the Mormons, and was called Carson county. It only became Nevada in 1861, by act of Congress. There is a popular tradition that God Almighty created it; but when you come to see it, William, you will think differently. Do not let that discourage you, though. The country looks something like a singed cat, owing to the scarcity of shrubbery, and also resembles that animal in the respect that it has more merits than its personal appearance would seem to indicate. The Grosch brothers found the first silver lead here in 1857. They also founded Silver City, I believe. (Observe the subtle joke, William.) But the "history" of Nevada which you demand, properly begins with the discovery of the Comstock lead, which event happened nearly five years ago. The opinion now prevailing in the East that the Comstock is on the Gould & Curry is erroneous; on the contrary, the Gould & Curry is on the Comstock. Please make the correction, William. Signify to your friends, also, that all the mines here do not pay dividends as yet; you may make this statement with the utmost unyielding inflexibility—it will not be contradicted from this quarter. The population of this Territory is about 35,000, one-half of which number reside in the united cities of Virginia and Gold Hill.

However, I will discontinue this history for the present, lest I get you too deeply interested in this distant land and cause you to neglect your family or your religion. But I will address you again upon the subject next year. In the meantime, allow me to answer your inquiry as to the character of our climate.

It has no character to speak of, William, and alas! in this respect it resembles many, ah, too many chambermaids in this wretched, wretched world. Sometimes we have the seasons in their regular order, and then again we have winter all the summer and summer all winter. Consequently, we have never yet come across an almanac that would just exactly fit this latitude. It is mighty regular about not raining, though, William. It will start in here in November and rain about four, and sometimes as much as seven days on a stretch; after that, you may loan out your umbrella for twelve months, with the serene confidence which a Christian feels in four aces. Sometimes the winter begins in November and winds up in June; and sometimes there is a bare suspicion of winter in March and April, and summer all the balance of the year. But as a general thing, William, the climate is good, what there is of it.

What are the productions of the earth? You mean in Nevada, of course. On our ranches here, anything can be raised that can be produced on the fertile fields of Missouri. But ranches are very scattering —as scattering, perhaps, as lawyers in heaven. Nevada, for the most part, is a barren waste of sand, embellished with melancholy sage-brush, and fenced in with snow-clad mountains. But these ghastly features were the salvation of the land, William, for no rightly constituted American would have ever come here if the place had been easy of access, and none of our pioneers would have staid after they got here if they had not felt satisfied that they could not find a smaller chance for making a living anywhere else. Such is man, William, as he crops out in America.

"Is it healthy?" Yes, I think it is as healthy here as it is in any part of the West. But never permit a question of that kind to vegetate in your brain, William, because as long as providence has an eye on you, you will not be likely to die until your time comes.

"What diseases do they die of mostly?" Well, they used to die of conical balls and cold steel, mostly, but here lately erysipelas and the intoxicating bowl have got the bugle on those things, as was very justly remarked by Mr. Rising last Sunday. I will observe, for your information, William, that Mr. Rising is our Episcopal minister, and has done as much as any man among us to redeem this community from its pristine state of semi-barbarism. We are afflicted with all the diseases incident to the same latitude in the States, I believe, with one or two added and half a dozen subtracted on account of our superior altitude. However, the doctors are about as successful here, both in killing and curing, as they are anywhere.

Now, as to whether it would be advisable for a man who can make a living in Missouri to emigrate to Nevada, I confess I am somewhat mixed. If you are not content in your present condition, it naturally follows that you would be entirely satisfied if you could make either more or less than a living. You would exult in the cheerful exhilaration always produced by a change. Well, you can find your opportunity here, where, if you retain your health, and are sober and industrious, you will inevitably make more than a living, and if you don't you won't. You can rely upon this statement, William. It contemplates any line of business except the selling of tracts. You cannot sell tracts here, William; the people take no interest in tracts; the very best efforts in the tract line—even with pictures on them—have met with no encouragement here. Besides, the newspapers have been interfering; a man gets his regular text or so from the Scriptures in his paper, along with the stock sales and the war news, every day, now. If you are in the tract business, William, take no chances on Washoe; but you can suceed at anything else here.

"I suppose you know Joel H. Smith?" Well—the fact is—I believe I don't. Now isn't that singular? Isn't it very singular? And he owns "considerable" in a mine here, too. Happy man. Actually owns in a mine here in Nevada Territory, and I never even heard of him. Strange—strange—do you know, William, it is the strangest thing that ever happened to me? And then he not only owns in a mine, but owns "considerable"; that is the strangest part about it—how a man could own considerable in a mine in Washoe and I not know anything about it. He is a lucky dog, though. But I strongly suspect that you have made a mistake in the name; I am confident you have; you mean John Smith—I know you do; I know it from the fact that he owns considerable in a mine here, because I sold him the property at a ruinous sacrifice on the very day he arrived here from over the plains. That man will be rich one of these days. I am just as well satisfied of it as I am of any precisely similar instance of the kind that has come under my notice. I said as much to him yesterday, and he said he was satisfied of it, also. But he did not say it with that air of triumphant exultation which a heart like mine so delights to behold in one to whom I have endeavored to be a benefactor in a small way. He looked pensive a while, but, finally, says he, "Do you know, I think I'd a been a rich man long ago if they'd ever found the d—d ledge?" That was my idea about it. I always thought, and I still think, that if they ever do find that ledge, his chances will be better than they are now. I guess Smith will be all right one of these centuries, if he keeps up his assessments—he is a young man yet.

Now, William, I have taken a liking to you, and I would like to sell you "considerable" in a mine in Washoe. I think I could get you a commanding interest in the "Union," Gold Hill, on easy terms. It is just the same as the "Yellow Jacket," which is one of the richest mines in the Territory. The title was in dispute between the two companies some two years ago, but that is all settled now. Let me hear from you on the subject. Greenbacks at par is as good a thing as I want. But seriously, William, don't you ever invest in a mining stock which you don't know anything about; beware of John Smith's experience.

You hope to hear from me soon? Very good. I shall also hope to hear from you soon, about that little matter above referred to. Now, William, ponder this epistle well; never mind the sarcasm, here and there, and the nonsense, but reflect upon the plain facts set forth, because they are facts and are meant to be so understood and believed.

Remember me affectionately to your friends and relations, and especially to your venerable grandmother, with whom I have not the pleasure to be acquainted—but that is of no consequence, you know. I have been in your town many a time, and all the towns of the neighboring counties—the hotel keepers will recollect me vividly. Remember me to them—I bear them no animosity.

Yours, affectionately,

MARK TWAIN.

The
MAN OF AFFAIRS

THE LAST NEVADA *territorial legislature met in Carson City, a few miles distant from the foot of Mount Davidson, in December, 1863. The* TERRITORIAL ENTERPRISE *sent Mark Twain down to report the proceedings. As the representative of the most influential newspaper in the territory, as the close friend of several politicians, and as the brother of the secretary to Governor Nye, he found himself a man of considerable importance. So popular was he that, after the legislature adjourned, a mock session, or Third House, convened and elected him its "governor." A. W. (Sandy) Baldwin and Theodore Winters, Washoe bigwigs mentioned in "Concerning Notaries," presented Mark Twain with a gold watch inscribed by his constituents "To Governor Mark Twain."*

Mark Twain's slight reference to his speaking in "A Tide of Eloquence" indicates that even before he presented his message to the Third House he was getting practice in forensics. More amusing, however, is his diatribe on seekers for the position of notary (was he thinking of John Phoenix's "Visit of the Inspector"?) who asked him to damn them with mild doses of his influence. In his list of applicants he mentions Judge Turner, notorious for taking bribes, Bill Stewart, shortly to be elected senator from the new state of Nevada, and Sandy Baldwin, well-known on the Comstock. The rest of the candidates are amusing principally through being found all in the same boat.

A TIDE OF ELOQUENCE

[MARK TWAIN, *the Washoe co-humorist with Dan de Quille on the* TERRITORIAL ENTERPRISE, *author of "How To Cure a Cold," the "Lick House Hop," the "Late Prize Fight," and such like wonderfully funny things in the* GOLDEN ERA, *lately attended a presentation affair at Virginia City, and distinguished himself—in his own words:*] Afterwards, Mr. Mark Twain being enthusiastically called upon, arose, and without previous preparation, burst forth in a tide of eloquence so grand, so luminous, so beautiful and so resplendent with the gorgeous fires of genius, that the audience were spell-bound by the magic of his words, and gazed in silent wonder in each other's faces as men who felt that they were listening to one gifted with inspiration. [Applause.] The proceedings did not end here, but at this point we deemed it best to stop reporting and go to dissipating, as the dread solitude of our position as a sober, rational Christian, in the midst of the drivelling and besotted multitude around us, had begun to shroud our spirits with a solemn sadness tinged with fear. At ten o'clock the curtain fell.

FROM THE *Golden Era,* DEC. 6, 1863. [T. E.]

CONCERNING NOTARIES

[*Mark Twain, the wild humorist of the Sage Brush Hills, writes from Carson City to the* TERRITORIAL ENTERPRISE, *telling all about the Legislature, Governor Nye, and the rest of mankind at Nevada's Capital. He says:*]

A strange, strange thing occurred here yesterday, to wit:

A MAN APPLIED FOR A NOTARY'S COMMISSION.

Think of it. Ponder over it. He wanted a notarial commission—he said so himself. He was from Storey county. He brought his little petition along with him. He brought it on two stages. It is voluminous. The County Surveyor is chaining it off. Three shifts of clerks will be employed night and day on it, deciphering the signatures and testing their genuineness. They began unrolling the petition at noon, and people of strong mining proclivities at once commenced locating claims on it. We are too late, you know. But then they say the extensions are just as good as the original. I believe you.

Since writing the above, I have discovered that the foregoing does not amount to much as a sensation item, after all. The reason is, because there are seventeen hundred and forty-two applications for notaryships already on file in the Governor's office. I was not aware of it, you know. There are also as much as eleven cords of petitions stacked up in his back yard. A watchman stands guard over this combustible material—the back yard is not insured.

Since writing the above, strange events have happened. I started downtown, and had not gone far, when I met a seedy, ornery, ratty, hang-dog-looking stranger, who approached me in the most insinuating manner, and said he was glad to see me. He said he had often sighed for an opportunity of becoming acquainted with me—that he had read my effusions (he called them "effusions,") with solemn delight, and had yearned to meet the author face to face. He said he was Billson—Billson of Lander—I might have heard of him. I told him I had—many a time —which was an infamous falsehood. He said "D—n it, old Quill-driver, you must come and take a drink with me"; and says I, "D—n it, old Vermin-ranch, I'll do it." [I had him there.] We took a drink, and he told the bar-keeper to charge it. After which, he opened a well-filled carpet-sack and took out a shirt-collar and a petition. He then threw the empty carpet-sack aside and unrolled several yards of the petition—"just for a starter," he said. "Now," says he, "Mark, have you got a good deal of influence with Governor Nye?" "Unbounded," says I, with honest pride; "when I go and use my influence with Governor Nye, and tell him it will be a great personal favor to me if he will do so and so, he always says it will be a real pleasure to him—that if it were any other man—any other man in the world—but seeing it's me, he wont." Mr. Billson then remarked that I was the very man; he wanted a little notarial appointment, and he would like me to mention it to the Governor. I said I would, and turned away, resolved to damn young Billson's official aspirations with a mild dose of my influence.

I walked about ten steps, and met a cordial man, with the dust of travel upon his garments. He mashed my hands in his, and as I stood straightening the joints back into their places again, says he, "Why darn it, Mark, how well you're looking! Thunder! It's been an age since I saw you. Turn around and let's look at you good. 'Gad, it's the same old Mark! Well, how've you been—and what have you been doing with yourself lately? Why don't you never come down and see a fellow ? Every time I come to town, the old woman's sure to get after me for not bringing you out, as soon as I get back. Why she takes them articles of yourn, and slathers 'em into her old scrap-book, along with deaths, and marriages, and receipts for the itch, and the small-pox, and hell knows what all, and if it warn't that you talk too slow to ever make love, dang my cats if I wouldn't be jealous of you. But what's the use fooling away time here?—let's go and gobble a cocktail." This was old Boreas, from Washoe. I went and gobbled a cocktail with him. He mentioned incidentally, that he wanted a notaryship, and showed me a good deal of his petition. I said I would use my influence in his behalf, and requested him to call at the Governor's office in the morning, and get his commission. He thanked me most heartily, and said he would. [I think I see him doing of it.]

I met another stranger before I got to the corner—a pompous little man with a crooked-handled cane and sorrel moustache. Says he, "How do you do, Mr. Twain—how do you do, sir? I am happy to see you, sir—

very happy indeed, sir. My name is——.Pardon me, sir, but I perceive you do not entirely recollect me—I am J. Bidlecome Dusenberry, of Esmeralda, formerly of the city of New York, sir." "Well," says I, "I'm glad to meet you, Dysentery, and—" "No, no—Dusenberry, sir, Dusenberry!—you—" "Oh, I beg your pardon," says I; "Dusenberry—yes, I understand, now; but it's all the same, you know—Dusenberry, by any other name would—however, I see you have a bale of dry goods—for me, perhaps." He said it was only a little petition, and proceeded to show me a few acres of it, observing casually that he was the candidate in the notarial line—that he had read my lucumbrations (he called it all that) with absorbing interest, and he would like me to use my influence with the Governor in his behalf. I assured him his commission would be ready for him as soon as it was signed. He appeared overcome with gratitude, and insisted, and insisted, and insisted, until at last I went and took a drink with him.

On the next corner I met Chief Justice Turner, on his way to the Governor's office with a petition. He said, "God bless you, my dear fellow—I'm delighted to see you—" and hurried on, after receiving my solemn promise that he should be a Notary Public if I could secure his appointment. Next I met William Stewart, grinning in his engaging way, and stroking his prodigious whiskers from his nose to his stomach. Sandy Baldwin was with him, and they both had measureless petitions on a dray with the names all signed in their own handwriting. I knew those fellows pretty well, and I didn't promise them my influence. I knew if the Governor refused to appoint them, they would have an injunction on him in less than twenty-four hours, and stop the issuance of any more Notary commissions. I met John B. Winters, next, and Judge North, and Mayor Arick, and Washoe Jim, and John O. Earl, and Ah Foo, and John H. Atchinson, and Hong Wo, and Wells Fargo, and Charley Strong, and Bob Morrow, and Gen. Williams, and seventy-two other prominent citizens of Storey county, with a long pack-train laden with their several petitions. I examined their documents, and promised to use my influence toward procuring notaryships for the whole tribe. I also drank with them.

I wandered down the street, conversing with every man I met, examining his petition. It became a sort of monomania with me, and I kept it up for two hours with unflagging interest. Finally, I stumbled upon a pensive, travel-worn stranger, leaning against an awning-post. I went up and looked at him. He looked at me. I looked at him again, and again he looked at me. I bent my gaze upon him once more, and says I, "Well?" He looked at me very hard, and says he, "Well—well what?" Says I, "Well—I would like to examine your petition, if you please."

He looked very much astonished—I may say amazed. When he had recovered his presence of mind, he says "What the devil do you mean?" I explained to him that I only wanted to glance over his petition for a notaryship. He said he believed I was a lunatic—he didn't like the unhealthy light in my eye, and he didn't want me to come any closer to him. I asked him if he had escaped the epidemic, and he shuddered and said he didn't know of any epidemic. I pointed to the large placard on the wall: "Coaches will leave the Ormsby House punctually every fifteen minutes, for the Governor's mansion, for the accommodation of Notarial aspirants, etc, etc.—Schemerhorn, Agent"—and I asked him if he didn't know enough to understand what that meant? I also pointed to the long procession of petition-laden citizens filing up the street toward the Governor's house, and asked him if he was not aware that all those fellows were going after notarial commissions—that the balance of the people had already gone, and that he and I had the whole town to ourselves ? He was astonished again. Then he placed his hand upon his heart, and swore a frightful oath that he had just arrived from over the mountains, and had no petition, and didn't want a notaryship. I gazed upon him a moment in silent rapture, and then clasped him to my breast. After which, I told him it was my turn to treat, by thunder. Whereupon, we entered a deserted saloon, and drank up its contents.We lay upon a billiard table in a torpid condition for many minutes, but at last my exile rose up and muttered in a sepulchral voice, "I feel it—O Heavens, I feel it in me veins!" "Feel what?" says I, alarmed. Says he, "I feel—O me sainted mother!—I feel—feel—a hankering to be a Notary Public!" And he tore down several yards of wall-paper, and fell to writing a petition on it. Poor devil—he had got it at last, and got it bad. I was seized with the fatal distemper a moment afterward. I wrote a petition with frantic haste, appended a copy of the Directory of Nevada Territory to it, and we fled down the deserted streets to the Governor's office.

But I must draw the curtain upon these harrowing scenes—the very memory of them scorches my brain. Ah, this Legislature has much to answer for in cutting down the number of Notaries Public in this Territory, with their infernal new law.

FROM THE *Golden Era*, FEB. 28, 1864. [T. E.]

III. LOCAL REPORTER IN SAN FRANCISCO

On
SAN FRANCISCO LOCALS

IN MAKING THE SHIFT *from Virginia City to San Francisco, Mark Twain was demoted to the position of city reporter. Shortly after his arrival in the Bay City in the early summer of 1864 he joined the staff of the* MORNING CALL. *The* CALL *was not as important a paper as either the morning* ALTA CALIFORNIA *or the* EVENING BULLETIN. *It was described by a contemporary as a "remarkably spirited and chatty little journal, published at a very cheap rate, having a large circulation, and being full of piquant paragraphs, bits of scandal, sensation 'items', and special scraps of news interesting to its numerous lady readers." It is not surprising that the restless individualist, forced into a daily routine and denied the opportunity to write as he pleased, broke his connections with the journal before the year was out.*

In the first of his Era sketches of this period we see Mark Twain living at Leland's newly-opened Occidental Hotel, famous for its cuisine and up-to-date furnishings. It was to hold its own as the leading San Francisco hotel until Ralston completed his Palace in the late sixties. Mention of the drop in value of Gould and Curry mining stock reminds us that speculation, litigation, and poor mining methods had brought temporary collapse to Virginia City silver production and permanent annihilation to Mark Twain's dream of becoming a silver nabob. Legend tells of the Washoe Giant's quip about the very modern-looking scissors in the Samson and Delilah picture which hung behind the bar in the Bank Exchange, but the original article is here reprinted for the first time. The Bank Exchange was the swankest saloon in the city; its appointments were described as "sumptuous without being meretriciously gaudy." The painting described by Mark Twain is said to have been a valuable art work imported from Europe; it is certain that the alluringly exposed Delilah was the only feminine presence allowed in this man's domain.

As a regular part of his "soulless drudgery" on the CALL *Mark spent an hour each morning in Judge Shepherd's police court listening to run-ins explain their squabbles of the night before. Burlesque of the circumlocutions of witnesses made a good subject for an* ERA *sketch, a by-product of an irksome job. In this item Mark Twain again toyed with the name Smith; because he liked to play with the name, from John Smith to Fitz Smythe, hardly an article on Smith could be written by a San Franciscan of the period without being attributed to Mark Twain. In his bibliography Merle Johnson thus errs in assigning several unsigned* ERA *articles about Smith-Brown-Jones to Mark Twain.*

Irritation at rising early was a typical subject for a humorist who devoted a surprisingly large amount of his early writing to cursing things that made him uncomfortable. Unfortunately, driving out to the Cliff House before breakfast was the fad of the summer, and Mark Twain could not escape it, although he confided to his note-book that the adage about the early bird getting the worm was an absurd saw. "I once knew a man who tried it. He got up at sunrise and a horse bit him." In "Early Rising" he agrees with Inigo, who also got up early to go to the Cliff House and as a result wrote: "Early rising is a practice based not so much upon the example of the lark as upon the reprehensible habit of the goose."*

IN THE METROPOLIS

To a christian who has toiled months and months in Washoe; whose hair bristles from a bed of sand, and whose soul is caked with a cement of alkali dust; whose nostrils know no perfume but the rank odor

* Quoted from Mark Twain's Note-book, HARPER'S, 1935, p. 12.

of sage-brush—and whose eyes know no landscape but barren mountains and desolate plains; where the winds blow, and the sun blisters, and the broken spirit of the contrite heart finds joy and peace only in Limberger cheese and lager beer—unto such a Christian, verily the Occidental Hotel is Heaven on the half shell. He may even secretly consider it to be Heaven on the entire shell, but his religion teaches a sound Washoe Christian that it would be sacrilege to say it.

Here you are expected to breakfast on salmon, fried oysters and other substantials, from 6 till half-past 12; you are required to lunch on cold fowl and so forth, from half-past 12 until 3; you are obliged to skirmish through a dinner comprising such edibles as the world produces, and keep it up, from 3 until half-past 7; you are then compelled to lay seige to the tea-table, from half-past 7 until 9 o'clock, at which hour, if you refuse to move upon the supper works and destroy oysters gotten up in all kinds of seductive styles, until 12 o'clock, the landlord will certainly be offended, and you might as well move your trunk to some other establishment. [It is a pleasure to me to observe, incidentally, that I am on good terms with the landlord yet.]

Why don't you send Dan down into the Gould & Curry mine, to see whether it has petered out or not, and if so, when it will be likely to peter in again. The extraordinary decline of that stock has given rise to the wildest surmises in the way of accounting for it, but among the lot there is harm in but one, which is the expressed belief on the part of a few that the bottom has fallen out of the mine. Gould & Curry is climbing again, however.

It has been many a day since San Francisco has seen livelier times in her theatrical department than at present. Large audiences are to be found nightly at the Opera House, the Metropolitan, the Academy of Music, the American, the New Idea, and even the Museum, which is not as good a one as Barnum's. The Circus company, also, played a lucrative engagement, but they are gone on their travels now. The graceful, charming, clipper-built Ella Zoyara was very popular.

Miss Caroline Richings has played during the past fortnight at Maguire's Opera House to large and fashionable audiences, and has delighted them beyond measure with her sweet singing. It sounds improbable, perhaps, but the statement is true, nevertheless.

You will hear of the Metropolitan, now, from every visitor to Washoe. It opened under the management of the new lessees, Miss Annette Ince and Julia Dean Hayne, with a company who are as nearly all stars as it was possible to make it. For instance—Annette Ince, Emily Jordan, Mrs. Judah, Julia Dean Hayne, James H. Taylor, Frank Lawlor,

Harry Courtaine and Fred. Franks (my favorite Washoe tragedian, whose name they have put in small letters in the programme, when it deserves to be in capitals—because, whatever part they give him to play don't he always play it well? and does he not possess the first virtue of a comedian, which is to do humorous things with grave decorum and without seeming to know that they are funny).

The birds, and the flowers, and the Chinamen, and the winds, and the sunshine, and all things that go to make life happy, are present in San Francisco to-day, just as they are all days in the year. Therefore, one would expect to hear these things spoken of, and gratefully, and disagreeable matters of little consequence allowed to pass without comment. I say, one would suppose that. But don't you deceive yourself—any one who supposes anything of the kind, supposes an absurdity. The multitude of pleasant things by which the people of San Francisco are surrounded are not talked of at all. No—they damn the wind, and they damn the dust, and they give all their attention to damning them well, and to all eternity. The blasted winds and the infernal dust—these alone form the eternal topics of conversation, and a mighty absurd topic it seems to one just out of Washoe. There isn't enough wind here to keep breath in my body, or dust enough to keep sand in my craw. But it is human nature to find fault—to overlook that which is pleasant to the eye, and seek after that which is distasteful to it. You take a stranger into the Bank Exchange and show him the magnificent picture of Samson and Delilah, and what is the first object he notices? — Samson's fine face and flaming eye? or the noble beauty of his form? or the lovely, half-nude Delilah? or the muscular Philistine behind Samson, who is furtively admiring her charms? or the perfectly counterfeited folds of the rich drapery below her knees? or the symmetry and truth to nature of Samson's left foot? No, sir, the first thing that catches his eye is the scissors on the floor at Delilah's feet, and the first thing he says, "Them scissors is too modern—there warn't no scissors like that in them days, by a d—d sight!"

FROM THE *Golden Era*, JUNE 26, 1864. [T. E.]

THE EVIDENCE

IN THE CASE OF SMITH vs JONES

I REPORTED THIS TRIAL simply for my own amusement, one idle day last week, and without expecting to publish any portion of it—but I have seen the facts in the case so distorted and misrepresented in the daily papers that I feel it my duty to come forward and do what I can to set the plaintiff and the defendant right before the public. This can best be done by submitting the plain, unembellished statements of the witnesses as given under oath before his Honor Judge Shepherd, in the Police Court, and leaving the people to form their own judgment of the matters involved, unbiased by argument or suggestion of any kind from me.

There is that nice sene of justice and that ability to discriminate between right and wrong, among the masses, which will enable them, after carefully reading the testimony I am about to set down here, to decide without hesitation which is the innocent party and which the guilty in the remarkable case of Smith vs. Jones, and I have every confidence that before this paper shall have been out of the printing-press twenty-four hours, the high court of The People, from whose decision there is no appeal, will have swept from the innocent man all taint of blame or suspicion, and cast upon the guilty one a deathless infamy.

To such as are not used to visiting the Police Court, I will observe that there is nothing inviting about the place, there being no rich carpets, no mirrors, no pictures, no elegant sofa or arm-chairs to lounge in, no free lunch—and, in fact, nothing to make a man who has been there once desire to go again—except in cases where his bail is heavier than his fine is likely to be, under which circumstances he naturally has a tendency in that direction again, of course, in order to recover the difference.

There is a pulpit at the head of the hall, occupied by a handsome gray-haired Judge, with a faculty of appearing pleasant and impartial to the disinterested spectator, and prejudiced and frosty to the last degree to the prisoner at the bar.

To the left of the pulpit is a long table for reporters; in front of the pulpit the clerks are stationed, and in the centre of the hall a nest of lawyers. On the left again are pine benches behind a railing, occupied by seedy white men, negroes, Chinaman, Kanakas—in a word, by the seedy and dejected of all nations—and in a corner is a box where more can be had when they are wanted.

On the right are more pine benches, for the use of prisoners, and their friends and witnesses.

An officer, in a gray uniform, and with a star upon his breast, guards the door.

A holy calm pervades the scene.

The case of Smith vs. Jones being called, each of these parties (stepping out from among the other seedy ones) gave the Court a particular and circumstantial account of how the whole thing occurred, and then sat down.

The two narratives differed from each other.

In reality, I was half persuaded that these men were talking about two separate and distinct affairs altogether, inasmuch as no single circumstance mentioned by one was even remotely hinted at by the other.

Mr. Alfred Sowerby was then called to the witness-stand, and testified as follows:

"I was in the saloon at the time, your honor, and I see this man Smith come up all of a sudden to Jones, who warn't saying a word, and split him in the snoot—"

Lawyer.—"Did what, Sir?"

Witness.—"Busted him in the snoot."

Lawyer.—"What do you mean by such language as that? When you say that the plaintiff suddenly approached the defendant, who was silent at the time, and 'busted him in the snoot,' do you mean that the plaintiff *struck* the defendant?"

Witness.—"That's me—I'm swearing to that very circumstance—yes, your honor, that was just the way of it. Now, for instance, as if you was Jones and I was Smith. Well, I comes up all of a sudden and says I to your Honor, says I, 'D—n your old tripe—,'" [Suppressed laughter in the lobbies.]

The Court.—"Order in the court! Witness, you will confine yourself to a plain statement of the facts in this case, and refrain from the embellishments of metaphor and allegory as far as possible."

Witness.—(Considerably subdued.)—"I beg your Honor's pardon—I didn't mean to be so brash. Well, Smith comes up to Jones all of a sudden and mashed him in the bugle—"

Lawyer.—"Stop! Witness, this kind of language will not do. I will ask you a plain question, and I require you to answer it simply, yes or no. Did—the—plaintiff—*strike*—the defendant? Did he *strike* him?"

Witness.—"You bet your sweet life he did. Gad! he gave him a paster in the trumpet—"

Lawyer.—"Take the witness! take the witness! take the witness! I have no further use for him."

The lawyer on the other side said he would endeavor to worry along without more assistance from Mr. Sowerby, and the witness retired to a neighboring bench.

Mr. McWilliamson was next called, and deposed as follows:

"I was a standing as close to Mr. Smith as I am to this pulpit, a-chaffing with one of the lager beer girls—Sophronia by name, being from summers in Germany, so she says, but as to that, I—"

Lawyer.—"Well, now, never mind the nativity of the lager beer girl, but state, as concisely as possible, what you know of the assault and battery."

Witness.—"Certainly—certainly. Well, German or no German,—which I'll take my oath I don't believe she is, being of a red-headed disposition, with long, bony fingers, and no more hankering after Limberger cheese than—"

Lawyer.—"Stop that driveling nonsense and stick to the assault and battery. Go on with your story."

Witness.—"Well, Sir, she—that is, Jones—he sidled up and drawed his revolver and tried to shoot the top of Smith's head off, and Smith run, and Sophronia she whalloped herself down in the saw-dust and screamed twice, just as loud as she could yell. I never see a poor creature in such distress—and then she sung out: 'O, H—ll's fire! what are they up to now? Ah, my poor dear mother, I shall never see you more!' —saying which, she jerked another yell and fainted away as dead as a wax figger. Thinks I to myself, I'll be danged if this ain't gettin' rather dusty, and I'll—"

The Court.—"We have no desire to know what you *thought*; we only wish to know what you *saw*. Are you sure Mr. Jones endeavored to shoot the top of Mr. Smith's head off?"

Witness.—"Yes, your Honor."

The Court.—"How many times did he shoot?"

Witness.—"Well, Sir, I couldn't say exactly as to the number—but I should think—well, say seven or eight times—as many as that, anyway."

The Court.—"Be careful now, and remember you are under oath. What kind of a pistol was it?"

Witness.—"It was a Durringer, your Honor."

The Court.—"A Deringer! You must not trifle here, Sir. A Deringer only shoots once—how then could Jones have fired seven or eight times?" [The witness is evidently as stunned by that last proposition as if a brick had struck him.]

Witness.—"Well, your Honor—he—that is, she—Jones, I mean—Soph—"

The Court.—"Are you sure he fired more than one shot? Are you sure he fired at all?"

Witness.—"I—I—well, perhaps he didn't—and—and your Honor may be right. But you see, that girl, with her dratted yowling—altogether, it might be that he did only shoot once."

Lawyer.—"And about his attempting to shoot the top of Smith's head off—didn't he aim at his body, or his legs? Come now."

Witness.—(entirely confused)—"Yes, Sir—I think he did—I—I'm pretty certain of it. Yes, Sir, he must a fired at his legs."

[Nothing was elicited on the cross examination, except that the weapon used by Mr. Jones was a bowie knife instead of a deringer, and that he made a number of desperate attempts to scalp the plaintiff instead of trying to shoot him. It also came out that Sophronia, of doubtful nativity, did not faint, and was not present during the affray, she having been discharged from her situation on the previous evening.]

Washington Billings, sworn, said:—"I see the row, and it warn't in no saloon—it was in the street. Both of 'em was drunk, and one was a comin' up the street, and 'tother was a goin' down. Both of 'em was close to the houses when they fust see each other, and both of 'em made their calculations to miss each other, but the second time they tacked across the pavement—driftin', like diagonal—they come together, down by the curb—almighty soggy, they did—which staggered 'em a moment, and then, over they went, into the gutter. Smith was up fust, and he made a dive for a cobble and fell on Jones; Jones dug out and made a dive for a cobble, and slipped his hold and jammed his head into Smith's stomach. They each done that over again, twice more, just the same way. After that, neither of 'em could get up any more, and so they just laid there in the slush and clawed mud and cussed each other."

[On the cross-examination, the witness could not say whether the parties continued the fight afterwards in the saloon or not—he only knew they began it in the gutter, and to the best of his knowledge and belief they were too drunk to get into a saloon, and too drunk to stay in it after they got there if there were any orifice about it that they could fall out of again. As to weapons, he saw none used except the cobble-stones, and to the best of his knowledge and belief they missed fire every time while he was present.]

Jeremiah Driscoll came forward, was sworn, and testified as follows: —"I saw the fight, your Honor, and it wasn't in a saloon, nor in the street, nor in a hotel, nor in—"

The Court.—"Was it in the City and County of San Francisco?"

Witness.—"Yes, your Honor, I—I think it was."

The Court.—"Well, then, go on."

Witness.—"It was up in the Square. Jones meets Smith, and they both go at it—that is, blackguarding each other. One called the other a thief, and the other said he was a liar, and then they got to swearing backwards and forwards pretty generally, as you might say, and finally one struck the other over the head with a cane, and then they closed and fell, and after that they made such a dust and the gravel flew so thick that I couldn't rightly tell which was getting the best of it. When it cleared away, one of them was after the other with a pine bench, and the other was prospecting for rocks, and—"

Lawyer.—"There, there, there—that will do—that—will—*do!* How in the world is any one to make head or tail out of such a string of nonsense as that? Who struck the first blow?"

Witness.—"I cannot rightly say, sir, but I think—"

Lawyer.—"You *think!*—don't you *know?*"

Witness.—"No, sir, it was all so sudden, and—"

Lawyer.—"Well, then, state, if you can, who struck the last."

Witness.—"I can't, sir, because—"

Lawyer.—"Because what?"

Witness.—"Because, sir, you see toward the last, they clinched and went down, and got to kicking up the gravel again, and—"

Lawyer.—(resignedly)—"Take the witness—take the witness."

[The testimony on the cross-examination went to show that during the fight, one of the parties drew a slung-shot and cocked it, but to the best of the witness' knowledge and belief, he did not fire; and at the same time, the other discharged a hand-grenade at his antagonist, which missed him and did no damage, except blowing up a bonnet store on the other side of the street, and creating a momentary diversion among the milliners. He could not say, however, which drew the slung-shot or which threw the grenade. (It was generally remarked by those in the court room, that the evidence of the witness was obscure and unsatisfactory.) Upon questioning him further, and confronting him with the parties to the case before the court, it transpired that the faces of Jones and Smith were unknown to him, and that he had been talking about an entirely different fight all the time.]

Other witnesses were examined, some of whom swore that Smith was the aggressor, and others that Jones began the row; some said they fought with their fists, others that they fought with knives, others tomahawks, others revolvers, others clubs, others axes, others beer mugs and chairs, and others swore there had been no fight at all. However, fight or no fight, the testimony was straightforward and uniform on one point, at any rate, and that was, that the fuss was about two dollars and forty cents, which one party owed the other, but after all, it was impossible to find out which was the debtor and which the creditor.

After the witnesses had all been heard, his Honor, Judge Shepherd, observed that the evidence in this case resembled, in a great many points, the evidence before him in some thirty-five cases every day, on an average. He then said he would continue the case, to afford the parties an opportunity of procuring more testimony.

[I have been keeping an eye on the Police Court for the last few days. Two friends of mine had business there, on account of assault and battery concerning Washoe stocks, and I felt interested, of course. I never knew their names were James Johnson and John Ward, though, until I heard them answer to them in that Court. When James Johnson was called, one of these young men said to the other: "That's you, my boy." "No," was the reply, "it's you—my name's John Ward—see, I've got it written here on a card." Consequently, the first speaker sung out, "Here!" and it was all right. As I was saying, I have been keeping an eye on the Court, and I have arrived at the conclusion that the office of Police Judge is a profitable and a comfortable thing to have, but then, as the English hunter said about fighting tigers in India under a shortness of ammunition, "it has its little drawbacks." Hearing testimony must be worrying to a Police Judge sometimes, when he is in his right mind. I would rather be Secretary to a wealthy mining company, and have nothing to do but advertise the assessments and collect them in carefully, and go along quiet and upright, and be one of the noblest works of God, and never gobble a dollar that didn't belong to me—all just as those fellows do, you know. (Oh, *I* have no talent for sarcasm, it isn't likely.) But I trespass.]

Now, with every confidence in the instinctive candor and fair dealing of my race, I submit the testimony in the case of Smith vs. Jones, to the People, without comment or argument, well satisfied that after a perusal of it, their judgment will be as righteous as it is final and impartial, and that whether Smith be cast out and Jones exalted, or Jones cast out and Smith exalted, the decision will be a holy and just one.

I leave the accused and the accuser before the bar of the world—let their fate be pronounced.

FROM THE *Golden Era*, JUNE 26, 1864.

EARLY RISING
AS REGARDS
EXCURSIONS TO THE CLIFF HOUSE

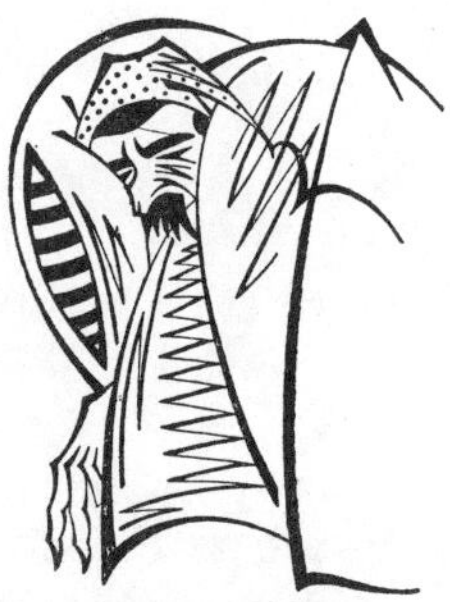

Early to bed, and early to rise,
Makes a man healthy, wealthy and wise.
—Benjamin Franklin.

I don't see it—George Washington.

Now BOTH OF THESE are high authorities—very high and respectable authorities—but I am with General Washington first, last, and all the time on this proposition.

Because I don't see it, either.

I have tried getting up early, and I have tried getting up late—and the latter agrees with me best. As for a man's growing any wiser, or any richer, or any healthier, by getting up early, I know it is not so; because

I have got up early in the station-house many and many a time, and got poorer and poorer for the next half a day, in consequence, instead of richer and richer. And sometimes, on the same terms, I have seen the sun rise four times a week up there at Virginia, and so far from my growing healthier on account of it, I got to looking blue, and pulpy, and swelled, like a drowned man, and my relations grew alarmed and thought they were going to lose me. They entirely despaired of my recovery, at one time, and began to grieve for me as one whose days were numbered—whose fate was sealed—who was soon to pass away from them forever, and from the glad sunshine, and the birds, and the odorous flowers, and murmuring brooks, and whispering winds, and all the cheerful scenes of life, and go down into the dark and silent tomb—and they went forth sorrowing, and jumped a lot in the graveyard, and made up their minds to grin and bear it with that fortitude which is the true Christian's brightest ornament.

You observe that I have put a stronger test on the matter than even Benjamin Franklin contemplated, and yet it would not work. Therefore, how is a man to grow healthier, and wealthier, and wiser by going to bed early and getting up early, when he fails to accomplish these things even when he does not go to bed at all? And as far as becoming wiser is concerned, you might put all the wisdom I acquired in these experiments in your eye, without obstructing your vision any to speak of.

As I said before, my voice is with George Washington's on this question.

Another philosopher encourages the world to get up at sunrise because "it is the early bird that catches the worm."

It is a seductive proposition, and well calculated to trap the unsuspecting. But its attractions are all wasted on me, because I have no use for the worm. If I had, I would adopt the Unreliable's plan. He was much interested in this quaint proverb, and directed the powers of his great mind to its consideration for three or four consecutive hours. He was supposing a case. He was supposing, for instance, that he really wanted the worm—that the possession of the worm was actually necessary to his happiness—that he yearned for it and hankered after it, therefore, as much as a man *could* yearn for and hanker after a worm under such circumstances—and he was supposing, further, that he was opposed to getting up early in order to catch it (which was much the more plausible of the two suppositions). Well, at the end of three or four hours' profound meditation upon the subject, the Unreliable rose up and said: "If he were so anxious about the worm, and he couldn't get along without him, and he didn't want to get up early in the morning to catch him—why then, by George, he would just lay for him the night before." I never would have thought of that. I looked at the youth, and said to myself, he is malicious, and dishonest, and unhandsome, and does not smell good—yet how quickly do these trivial demerits disappear in the shadow, when the glare from this great intellect shines out above them!

I have always heard that the only time in the day that a trip to the Cliff House could be thoroughly enjoyed was early in the morning (and I suppose it might be as well to withhold an adverse impression while the flow-tide of public opinion continues to set in that direction.)

I tried it the other morning with Harry, the stock-broker, rising at 4 A.M., to delight in the following described things, to wit:

A road unencumbered by carriages, and free from wind and dust; a bracing atmosphere; the gorgeous spectacle of the sun in the dawn of his glory; the fresh perfume of flowers still damp with dew; a solitary drive on the beach while its smoothness was yet unmarred by wheel or hoof, and a vision of white sails glinting in the morning light far out at sea.

These were the considerations, and they seemed worthy a sacrifice of seven or eight hours' sleep.

We sat in the stable, and yawned, and gaped, and stretched, until the horse was hitched up, and then drove out into the bracing atmosphere. (When another early voyage is proposed to me, I want it understood that there is to be no bracing atmosphere in the programme. I can worry along without it.) In half an hour we were so thoroughly braced up with it that it was just a scratch that we were not frozen to death. Then the harness came unshipped, or got broken, or something, and I waxed colder and drowsier while Harry fixed it. I am not fastidious about clothes, but I am not used to wearing fragrant, sweaty horse-blankets, and not partial to them, either; I am not proud, though, when I am freezing, and I added the horse-blanket to my overcoats, and tried to wake up and feel warm and cheerful. It was useless, however—all my senses slumbered and continued to slumber, save the sense of smell.

When my friend drove past suburban gardens and said the flowers never exhaled so sweet an odor before, in his experience, I dreamily but honestly endeavored to think so too, but in my secret soul I was conscious that they only smelled like horse-blankets. (When another early voyage is proposed to me, I want it understood that there is to be no "fresh perfume of flowers" in the programme, either. I do not enjoy it. My senses are not attuned to the flavor—there is too much horse about it and not enough eau de cologne.)

The wind was cold and benumbing, and blew with such force that we could hardly make headway against it. It came straight from the ocean, and I think there are icebergs out there somewhere. True, there was not much dust, because the gale blew it all to Oregon in two minutes; and by good fortune, it blew no gravel-stones, to speak of—only one of any consequence, I believe—a three-cornered one—it struck me in the eye. I have it there yet. However, it does not matter—for the future I suppose I can manage to see tolerably well out of the other. (Still, when another early voyage is proposed to me, I want it understood that the dust is to be put in, and the gravel left out of the programme. I might want my other eye if I continue to hang on until my time comes; and besides, I shall not mind the dust much hereafter, because I have only got to shut one eye, now, when it is around.)

No, the road was not encumbered by carriages—we had it all to ourselves. I suppose the reason was, that most people do not like to enjoy themselves too much, and therefore they do not go out to the Cliff House in the cold and the fog, and the dread silence and solitude of four o'clock in the morning. They are right. The impressive solemnity of such a pleasure trip is only equalled by an excursion to Lone Mountain in a hearse. Whatever of advantage there may be in having that Cliff House road all to yourself we had—but to my mind a greater advantage would be in dividing it up in small sections among the entire community; because, in consequence of the repairs in progress on it just now, it's as rough as a corduroy bridge—(in a good many places) and consequently the less you have of it, the happier you are likely to be and the less shaken up and disarranged on the inside. (Wherefore, when another early voyage is proposed to me, I want it understood that the road is not to be unencumbered with carriages, but just the reverse—so that the balance of the people shall be made to stand their share of the jolting and the desperate lonesomeness of the thing.)

From the moment we left the stable, almost, the fog was so thick that we could scarcely see fifty yards behind or before, or overhead; and for a while, as we approached the Cliff House, we could not see the horse at all, and were obliged to steer by his ears, which stood up dimly out of the dense white mist that enveloped him. But for those friendly beacons, we must have been cast away and lost.

I have no opinion of a six-mile ride in the clouds; but if I ever have to take another, I want to leave the horse in the stable and go in a balloon. I shall prefer to go in the afternoon, also, when it is warm, so that I may gape, and yawn, and stretch, if I am drowsy, without disarranging my horse-blanket and letting in a blast of cold wind.

We could scarcely see the sportive seals out on the rocks, writhing and squirming like exaggerated maggots, and there was nothing soothing in their discordant barking, to a spirit so depressed as mine was.

Harry took a cocktail at the Cliff House, but I scorned such ineffectual stimulus; I yearned for fire, and there was none there; they were about to make one, but the bar-keeper looked altogether too cheerful for me—I could not bear his unnatural happiness in the midst of such a ghastly picture of fog, and damp, and frosty surf, and dreary solitude. I could not bear the sacrilegious presence of a pleasant face at such a time; it was too much like sprightliness at a funeral, and we fled from it down the smooth and vacant beach.

We had that all to ourselves, too, like the road—and I want it divided up, also, hereafter. We could not drive in the roaring surf and seem to float abroad on the foamy sea, as one is wont to do in the sunny afternoon, because the very thought of any of that icy-looking water splashing on you was enough to congeal your blood, almost. We saw no white-winged ships sailing away on the billowy ocean, with the pearly light of morning descending upon them like a benediction—"because the fog had the bulge on the pearly light," as the Unreliable observed when I mentioned it to him afterwards; and we saw not the sun in the dawn of his glory, for the same reason. Hill and beach, and sea and sun were all wrapped in a ghostly mantle of mist, and hidden from our mortal vision. (When another early voyage is proposed to me, I want it understood that the sun in his glory, and the morning light, and the ships at sea, and all that sort of thing are to be left out of the programme, so that when we fail to see them, we shall not be so infernally disappointed.)

We were human icicles when we got to the Ocean House, and there was no fire there, either. I banished all hope, then, and succumbed to despair; I went back on my religion, and sought surcease of sorrow in soothing blasphemy. I am sorry I did it, now, but it was a great comfort to me, then. We could have had breakfast at the Ocean House, but we did not want it; can statues of ice feel hunger? But we adjourned to a private room and ordered red-hot coffee, and it was a sort of balm to my troubled mind to observe that the man who brought it was as cold, and as silent, and as solemn as the grave itself. His gravity was so impressive, and so appropriate and becoming to the melancholy surroundings, that it won upon me and thawed out some of the better instincts of my nature, and I told him he might ask a blessing if he thought it would lighten him up any—because he looked as if he wanted to, very bad—but he only shook his head resignedly and sighed.

That coffee did the business for us. It was made by a master artist, and it had not a fault; and the cream that came with it was so rich and thick that you could hardly have strained it through a wire fence. As the generous beverage flowed down our frigid throats, our blood grew warm again, our muscles relaxed, our torpid bodies awoke to life and feeling, anger and uncharitableness departed from us and we were cheerful once more. We got good cigars, also, at the Ocean House, and drove into town over a smooth road, lighted by the sun and unclouded by fog.

Near the Jewish cemeteries we turned a corner too suddenly, and got upset, but sustained no damage, although the horse did what he honestly could to kick the buggy out of the State while we were grovelling in the sand. We went on down to the steamer and while we were on board, the buggy was upset again by some outlaw, and an axle broken.

However, these little accidents, and all the deviltry and misfortune that preceded them, were only just and natural consequences of the absurd experiment of getting up at an hour in the morning when all God-fearing Christians ought to be in bed. I consider that the man who leaves his pillow, deliberately, at sun-rise, is taking his life in his own hands, and he ought to feel proud if he don't have to put it down again at the coroner's office before dark.

Now, for that early trip, I am not any healthier or any wealthier than I was before, and only wiser in that I know a good deal better than to go and do it again. And as for all those notable advantages, such as the sun in the dawn of his glory, and the ships, and the perfume of the flowers, etc., etc., etc., I don't see them, any more than myself and Washington see the soundness of Benjamin Franklin's attractive little poem.

If you go to the Cliff House at any time after seven in the morning, you cannot fail to enjoy it—but never start out there before daylight, under the impression that you are going to have a pleasant time and come back insufferably healthier and wealthier and wiser than your betters on account of it. Because if you do you will miss your calculation, and it will keep you swearing about it right straight along for a week, to get even again.

Put no trust in the benefits to accrue from early rising, as set forth by the infatuated Franklin—but stake the last cent of your substance on the judgment of old George Washington, the Father of his Country, who said "he couldn't see it."

And you hear me endorsing that sentiment.

FROM THE *Golden Era*, JULY 3, 1864.

The
EARTHQUAKE OF 1865

WHEN MARK TWAIN *in* ROUGHING IT *said that an earthquake stirred him out of his lethargy during the fall of '64, when he was working for the* CALL *and still expecting to grow wealthy from Washoe silver, his memory for dates was playing him false. The quake he described took place on October 8th, 1865, nearly a year after he left the* CALL. *Except for two winter months spent in the Mother Lode country listening to Jim Gillis and Ross Coon spin yarns, he had spent that year in San Francisco corresponding regularly for the* TERRITORIAL ENTERPRISE *and writing articles almost weekly for the* CALIFORNIAN. *For some time the* GOLDEN ERA *had carried none of his work, but after the shake-up, it reprinted his "Earthquake Almanac," which had first appeared in the* DRAMATIC CHRONICLE. *The DeYoung brothers not long before had started the Dramatic Chronicle as a free theatre program; soon their policy of getting local writers to contribute to it brought it so much popularity that they turned it into a genuine newspaper, the San Francisco Chronicle.*

Although the earthquake of '65 did no great damage, it aroused a good deal of apprehension and discussion among the populace. The quake came early on a Sunday morning when many were in church and still more were at home, sleeping. The fronts of a few buildings crumpled, many windows and dishes were smashed, and—acording to Mark Twain—a crack over a hundred feet long gaped in the middle of a main street for a minute, and then closed forever. Most anecdotes of this quake concern preachers reaching the front door before their congregation, church-going citizens emerging from saloons, and late sleepers appearing on the street in various degrees of nakedness.

Mark Twain, in deploring the failure of the almanacs to forecast the event, tried his hand at suggesting the time for the next quake. He anticipated it would follow in just one month. It actually took three years to arrive, turning up on the 21st of October, 1868. When San Francisco was shaken for the second time in the sixties, Bret Harte, then editor of the OVERLAND MONTHLY, *made himself very unpopular by commenting on the catastrophe in his editorials. Thus, he was one of the first California editors to suggest that it is better to build for earthquakes than to ignore them.*

EARTHQUAKE ALMANAC

AT THE INSTANCE of several friends who feel a boding anxiety to know beforehand what sort of phenomena we may expect the elements to exhibit during the next month or two, and who have lost all confidence in the various patent medicine almanacs, because of the unaccountable reticence of those works concerning the extraordinary event of the 8th inst., I have compiled the following almanac expressly for this latitude:

Oct. 17.—Weather hazy; atmosphere murky and dense. An expression of profound melancholy will be observable upon most countenances.

Oct. 18.—Slight earthquake. Countenances grow more melancholy.

Oct. 19.—Look out for rain. It would be absurd to look in for it. The general depression of spirits increased.

Oct. 20.—More weather.

Oct. 21.—Same.

Oct. 22.—Light winds, perhaps. If they blow, it will be from the "east'ard, or the nor'ard, or the west'ard, or the suth'ard," or from some general direction approximating more or less to these points of the compass or otherwise. Winds are uncertain—more especially when they blow from whence they cometh and whither they listeth. N. B.—Such is the nature of winds.

Oct. 23.—Mild, balmy earthquakes.

Oct. 24.—Shaky.

Oct. 25.—Occasional shakes, followed by light showers of bricks and plastering. N. B.—Stand from under.

Oct. 26.—Considerable phenomenal atmospheric foolishness. About this time expect more earthquakes, but do not look out for them, on acount of the bricks.

Oct. 27.—Universal despondency, indicative of approaching disaster. Abstain from smiling, or indulgence in humorous conversation, or exasperating jokes.

Oct. 28.—Misery, dismal forebodings and despair. Beware of all light discourse—a joke uttered at this time would produce a popular outbreak.

Oct. 29.—Beware!

Oct. 30.—Keep dark!

Oct. 31.—Go slow!

Nov. 1.—Terrific earthquake. This is the great earthquake month. More stars fall and more worlds are slathered around carelessly and destroyed in November than in any other month of the twelve.

Nov. 2.—Spasmodic but exhilarating earthquakes, accompanied by occasional showers of rain, and churches and things.

Nov. 3.—Make your will.

Nov. 4.—Sell out.

Nov. 5.—Select your "last words." Those of John Quincy Adams will do, with the addition of a syllable, thus: "This is the last of earthquakes."

Nov. 6.—Prepare to shed this mortal coil.

Nov. 7.—Shed.

Nov. 8.—The sun will rise as usual, perhaps; but if he does he will doubtless be staggered some to find nothing but a large round hole eight thousand miles in diameter in the place where he saw this world serenely spinning the day before.

FROM THE *Golden Era*, OCT. 22, 1865.
REPRINTED FROM THE SAN FRANCISCO *Dramatic Chronicle*

IV. SAN FRANCISCO EXPLAINED TO WASHOE

San Francisco EXPLAINED *to* WASHOE

DURING MARK TWAIN'S last months in San Francisco, the GOLDEN ERA made a policy of reprinting the most interesting of his daily letters to the TERRITORIAL ENTERPRISE. Probably this exchange was made under an arrangement between the author and the San Francisco and Virginia City journals.

For the convenience of the reader the following thirteen items are grouped roughly according to their subjects. The first concerns feuds—one with the city administration and one with a rival journalist. Although biographers have noted that Mark Twain launched a campaign of ridicule against the local police, an attack which at least once caused him personal inconvenience, none of his thrusts have heretofore been reprinted. His grievance this time is that the police beat up a man caught stealing some flour-sacks and then so neglected him in jail that he died from their treatment.

Little of the genuine indignation which prompted the attack on a corrupt administration, however, motivated the famous feud with Fitz Smythe, which started as a personal tiff and ended as a tradition. A reporter on the ALTA CALIFORNIA, presumably the Mr. Evans mentioned by Paine in his biography, was ridiculed by Mark Twain for overwriting his local items. The reporters on the CALL were always poking fun at the sententious tone of the "Daily Morning Blanket," as they called the ALTA, and if Evans had not been singled out to be "Fitz Smythe" another man would have been. After attaching the new name to his man Mark Twain attributed to him a poem on Lincoln's death which included the lines "Gone, gone, gone. Forever and forever." In criticizing Fitz Smythe's real or putative elegy he remarked that the poet had used "a little too much gone and not enough forever." Fitz Smythe was at other times pictured swapping lies with Ananias on the outskirts of hell, posing in full uniform as secretary to Emperor Norton, and feeding his unfortunate horse solely on old issues of the ALTA and the BULLETIN.

Tradition has it that the steed chose starvation in preference to continuing this wretched diet.

The theatre items include a warning to the famous tragedian, Edwin Forrest, to expect no kind words from the self-conscious San Francisco critics, and a comment on the toughness and longevity of the Chapman family, occasioned by the apearance of Caroline Chapman in NEIGHBOR JACKWOOD *at the American Theatre. Members of the family had been favorites of the frontier stage both on the Mississippi show-boats and in early El Dorado; although she was well past her prime, San Francisco greeted Caroline with real affection as the last survivor of the troupe.*

News from the war-torn South doubtless prompted the comment on a fellow river-pilot, Captain Montgomery, who may have figured in the dispatches; and an item about a newspaper correspondent joining a Siberian engineering project suggested the short treatise on salmon economy. The burlesque biography of George Washington is valuable principally to show how badly even Mark Twain wrote when he was expected to be funny just because the 22nd of February had come around again.

That Virginia City continued to suffer hard times is indicated both by the item titled "Busted, and Gone Abroad," and the account of the stingy millionaire who set his friends up to a beer apiece. The nabobs and the bonanza kings were retrenching. On the other hand Mark Twain warned his less pretentious friends that "bumming" in the city hotels was not what it had been (but let's not take him too seriously).

Finally, Mark Twain, grumbling again at a world of petty annoyances, protests about New Year's calling, about useless shoe-shines, and about serious sermons. His "Reflections on the Sabbath" show him at his best, kidding Reverend Wadsworth, star of the Presbyterian Church and one of the most spectacular pulpit orators in a city which went in for that sort of thing. A visitor said of Wadsworth: "He has the real grit in him and makes an awful pile of rocks." Mark Twain refers to his own campaign against Sunday-school stories about good and bad little boys which he had already started and which he was to continue until it culminated in TOM SAWYER *and* HUCKLEBERRY FINN; *he calls himself a "Brevet Presbyterian," with adequate explanation of what that rank means; and he compares the old reliables and the wildcat religions, chief of which was spiritualism, the rage of the day. Accounts of his investigation of the spiritualists are reserved for another section.*

WHAT HAVE THE POLICE BEEN DOING?

AIN'T THEY virtuous? Don't they take good care of the city? Is not their constant vigilance and efficiency shown in the fact that roughs and rowdies here are awed into good conduct?—isn't it shown in the fact that ladies even on the back streets are safe from insult in the daytime, when they are under the protection of a regiment of soldiers?—isn't it shown in the fact that although many offenders of importance go unpunished, they infallibly snaffle every Chinese chicken-thief that attempts to drive his trade, and are duly glorified by name in the papers for it?—isn't it shown in the fact that they are always on the look-out and keep out of the way and never get run over by wagons and things? And ain't they spry?—ain't they energetic?—ain't they frisky?—Don't they parade up and down the sidewalk at the rate of a block an hour and make everybody nervous and dizzy with their frightful velocity? Don't they keep their clothes nice—and ain't their hands soft? And don't they work?—don't they work like horses?—don't they, now? Don't they smile sweetly on the women?—and when they are fatigued with their exertions, don't they back up against a lamp-post and go on smiling till they break plum down? But ain't they nice?—that's it, you know!—ain't they nice? They don't sweat—you never see one of those fellows sweat. Why, if you were to see a policeman sweating you would say, "oh, here, this poor man is going to die—because this sort of thing is unnatural, you know." Oh, no—you never see one of those fellows sweat. And ain't they easy and comfortable and happy—always leaning up against a lamp-post in the sun, and scratching one shin with the other foot and enjoying themselves? Serene?—I reckon not.

I don't know anything the matter with the Department, but may be Dr. Rowell does. Now when Ziele broke that poor wretch's skull the other night for stealing six bits' worth of flour sacks, and had him taken to the Station House by a policeman, and jammed into one of the cells in the most humorous way, do you think there was anything wrong there? I don't. Why should they arrest Ziele and say, "Oh, come, now, you *say* you found this stranger stealing on your premises, and we know you knocked him on the head with your club—but then you better go in a cell, too, till we see whether there's going to be any other account of the thing—any account that mightn't jibe with yours altogether, you know—you go in for confessed assault and battery, you know." Why should they do that? Well, nobody ever said they did.

And why shouldn't they shove that half-senseless wounded man into a cell without getting a doctor to examine and see how badly he was hurt, and consider that next day would be time enough, if he chanced to live that long? And why shouldn't the jailor let him alone when he found him in a dead stupor two hours after—let him alone because he coudn't wake him—couldn't wake a man who was sleeping and with that calm serenity which is peculiar to men whose heads have been caved in with a club—couldn't wake such a subject, but never suspected that there was anything unusual in the circumstance? Why shouldn't the jailor do so? Why certainly—why shouldn't he?—the man was an infernal stranger. He had no vote. Besides, had not a gentleman just said he stole some flour sacks? Ah, and if he stole flour sacks, did he not deliberately put himself outside the pale of humanity and Christian sympathy by that hellish act? I think so. The Department think so. Therefore, when the stranger died at 7 in the morning, after four hours of refreshing slumber in that cell, with his skull actually split in twain from front to rear, like an apple, as was ascertained by post mortem examination, what the very devil do you want to go and find fault with the prison officers for? You are *always* putting in your shovel. Can't you find somebody to pick on besides the police? It takes all my time to defend them from people's attacks.

I know the Police Department is a kind, humane and generous institution. Why, it was no longer ago than yesterday that I was reminded of that time Captain Lees broke his leg. Didn't the free-handed, noble Department shine forth with a dazzling radiance then? Didn't the Chief detail officers Shields, Ward and two others to watch over him and nurse him and look after all his wants with motherly solicitude—four of them, you know—four of the very biggest and ablest-bodied men on the force—when less generous people would have thought two nurses sufficient—had these four acrobats in active hospital service that way in the most liberal manner, at a cost to the city of San Francisco of only the trifling sum of five hundred dollars a month—the same being the salaries of four officers of the regular police force at $125 a month each. But don't you know there are people mean enough to say that Captain Lees ought to have paid his own nurse bills, and that if he had had to do it may be he would have managed to worry along on less than five hundred dollars worth of nursing a month? And don't you know that they say also that interested parties are always badgering the Supervisors with petitions for an increase of the police force, and showing such increase to be a terrible necessity, and yet they have always got to be hunting up and creating new civil offices and berths, and making details for nurse service in order to find something for them to do after they get them appointed? And don't you know that they say that they wish to God the city would hire a detachment of nurses and keep them where they will be handy in case of accident, so that property will not be left unprotected while policemen are absent on duty in sick rooms. You can't think how it aggravates me to hear such harsh remarks about our virtuous police force. Ah, well, the police will have their reward hereafter —no doubt.

FROM THE *Golden Era*, JAN. 21, 1866. [T.E.]

FITZ SMYTHE'S HORSE

YESTERDAY, as I was coming along through a back alley, I glanced over a fence, and there was Fitz Smythe's horse. I can easily understand, now, why that horse always looks so dejected and indifferent to the things of this world. They feed him on old newspapers. I had often seen Smythe carrying "dead loads" of old exchanges up town, but I never suspected that they were to be put to such a use as this. A boy came up while I stood there, and said: "That hoss belongs to Mr. Fitz Smythe, and the old man—that's my father, you know—the old man's going to kill him."

"Who, Fitz Smythe?"

"No, the hoss—because he et up a litter of pups that the old man wouldn't a taken forty dol—"

"Who, Fitz Smythe?"

"No, the hoss—and he eats fences and everything—took our gait off and carried it home and et up every dam splinter of it; you wait till he gets done with them old *Altas* and *Bulletins* he's a chawin' on now, and you'll see him branch out and tackle a-n-y-thing he can shet his mouth on. Why, he nipped a little boy, Sunday, which was going home from Sunday school; well, the boy got loose, you know, but that old hoss got his bible and some tracts, and them's as good a thing as *he* wants, being so used to papers, you see. You put anything to eat anywheres, and that old hoss'll shin out and get it—and he'll eat anything he can bite, and he don't care a dam. He'd climb a tree, he would, if you was to put anything up there for him—cats, for instance—he likes cats—he's et up every cat there was here in four blocks—he'll take more chances—why, he'll bust in anywheres for one of them fellers; I see him snake a old tom cat out of them there flower-pot over yonder, where she was a sunning of herself, and take her down, and she a hanging on and grabbing for a holt on something, and you could hear her yowl and kick up and tear around after she was inside of him. You see Mr. Fitz Smythe don't give him nothing to eat but them old newspapers and sometimes a basket of shavings, and so you know, he's got to prospect or starve, and a hoss ain't going to starve, it ain't likely, on account of not wanting to be rough on cats and sich things. Not that hoss, anyway, you bet you. Because *he* don't care a dam. You turn him loose once on this town, and don't you know he'd eat up m-o-r-e goods-boxes, and fences, clothing-store things, and animals, and all them kind of valuables? Oh, you bet he would. Because, that's his style, you know, and he don't care a dam. But you ought to see Mr. Fitz Smythe ride him around, prospecting for them items—you ought to see him with his soldier coat on, and his mustashers sticking out strong like a cat-fish's horns, and them long legs of his'n standing out so, like them two prongs they prop up a step-ladder with, and a jolting down street at four mile a week—oh, what a guy!—sets up stiff like a close pin, you know, and thinks he looks like old General Macdowl. But the old man's going to horniss-woggle that hoss on account of his gobbling up them pups. Oh, you bet your life the old man's *down* on him. Yes, sir, coming!" and the entertaining boy departed to see what the "old man" was calling him for. But I am glad that I met the boy, and I am glad I saw the horse taking his literary breakfast, because I know now why the animal looks so discouraged when I see Fitz Smythe rambling down Montgomery street on him—he has altogether too rough a time getting a living to be cheerful and frivolous or anyways frisky.

FROM THE *Golden Era*, JAN. 21, 1866. [T. E.]

ON CALIFORNIA CRITICS

EDWIN FORREST is coming here. Very well—good bye, Mr. Forrest. Our critics will make you sing a lively tune. They will soon let you know that your great reputation cannot protect you on this coast. You have passed muster in New York, but they will show you up here. They will make it very warm for you. They will make you understand that a man who has served a lifetime as dramatic critic on a New York paper may still be incompetent, but that a California critic knows it all, notwithstanding he may have been in the shoemaking business most of his life, or a plow-artist on a ranch. You will be the sickest man in America before you get through with this trip. They will set up Frank Mayo for your model as soon as you get here, and they will say you don't play up to him, whether you do or not. And then they will decide that you are a "bilk." That is the grand climax of all criticism. They will say it here, first, and the country papers will endorse it afterwards. It will then be considered proven. You might as well as quit, then.

You see, they always go into ecstatsies with an actor the first night he plays, and they call him the most gifted in America the next morning. Then they think they have not acted with metropolitan coolness and self possession, and they slew around on the other tack and abuse him like a pickpocket to get even. This was Bandman's experience, Menken's, Heron's, Vestali's, Boniface's, and many others I could name. It will be yours also. You had better stay where you are. You will regret it if you come here. How would you feel if they told you your playing might answer in places of small consequence but wouldn't do in San Francisco? They will tell you that, as sure as you live. And then say, in the most crushing way:

"Mr. Forrest has evidently mistaken the character of this people. We will charitably suppose that this is the case, at any rate. We make no inquiry as to what kind of people he has been in the habit of playing before, but we simply inform him that he is now in the midst of a refined and cultivated community, and one which will not tolerate such indelicate allusions as were made use of in the play of 'Othello' last night. If he would not play to empty benches, this must not be repeated." They always come the "refined and cultivated" dodge on a new actor—look out for it, Mr. Forrest, and do not let it floor you. The boys know enough that it is one of the most effective shots that can be fired at a stranger. Come on, Forrest—I will write your dramatic obituary, gratis.

FROM THE *Golden Era*, FEB. 25, 1866.

THE CHAPMAN FAMILY

THE OLD GENTLEMAN and the old lady must be seventy-five years old, now. They used to play with Dan. Marble in New Orleans, twenty-five years ago; earlier, they had a theatre built in a "broad horn," and floated down the Ohio and Mississippi clear to the Belize, tying up every night and knocking Richard III endways for the delectation of any number of graybacks that chose to come, from a dozen to a thousand, and selling tickets for money when they could, and taking Salt Lake currency when they couldn't. They have played in Canada and all over California and Washoe—played everywhere in North America, I may say, and lo! I come to tell you that they still "keep up their lick." I have been honored with a letter from the old lady, dated "Helena, Last Chance, Montana Territory, December 16." She says that they are just five miles from the Missouri river. I suppose they will build a raft in the spring and float down the river, astonishing the Indians with Othello, Richard, Jack Sheppard, etc., and the next thing we hear of them they will be in New Orleans again. The old lady further says:

"We have a theatre and company of Denverites, and are doing well. It is so cold that the quicksilver all froze, or I would tell you how many degrees below zero. Provisions high; salt, $1 per lb; butter, $2.50; flour, $30, and it would not do for you to be here, for tobacco is $6 a pound and scarce.*** So cold that 50 head of cattle and 2 men who were herding them froze to death on the night of the 14th. Great deal of suffering among miners who were out prospecting. This is a lively town; adjoining camps deserted; everybody wintering here.*** I play the part of Richard III tonight. Next week I appear as Mazeppa. We charge $1.50 for all seats."

The idea of the jolly, motherly old lady stripping to her shirt and riding a fiery untamed Montana jackass up flights of stairs and kicking up and cavorting around the stage on him with the quicksilver frozen in the thermometers and the audience taking brandy punches out of their pockets and biting them, same as people eat peanuts in civilized lands! Why, there is no end to the old woman's energy. She'll go through with Mazeppa with flying colors even if she has to do it with icicles a yard long hanging to her jackass's tail.

FROM THE *Golden Era*, JAN. 28, 1866.

CAPTAIN MONTGOMERY

WHENEVER he commenced helping anybody, Captain Ed. Montgomery never relaxed his good offices as long as help was needed.

As soon as he found that no steamboat ever stopped to wood with old Mother Utterback in the bend below Grand Gulf, Mississippi, and that she was poor and needed assistance, he began to stop there every trip and take her little pile of wood and smile grimly, when the engineers protested that it wouldn't burn any more than so many icicles—and stop there again the very next trip. He used to go ashore and talk to the old woman, and it flattered her to the last degree to be on such sociable terms with the high chief officer of a splendid passenger steamer. She would welcome him to her shabby little floorless log cabin with a royal flourish, and make her six gawky "gals" fly around and make him comfortable. He used to bring his lady passengers ashore to be entertained with Mother Utterback's quaint conversation.

I do not know that this incident is worth recording, but still, as it may let in the light of instruction to some darkened mind, I will just set down the circumstances of one of Captain Montgomery's visits to Mother Utterback and her daughters. He brought some fine ladies with him to enjoy the old woman's talk.

"Good morning, Captain Montgomery!" said she with many a bustling bow and flourish; "Good morning, Captain Montgomery; good morning, ladies all; how de do, Captain Montgomery—how de do—how de do? Sakes alive, it 'pears to me it's ben years sense I seed you. Fly around, gals, fly around! You Bets, you slut, highst yoself off'n that candle-box and give it to the lady. How *have* you ben, Captain Montgomery?—make yoself at home, ladies all—you 'Liza Jane, stan' out of the way—move yoself! Thar's the jug, help yoself, Captain Montgomery; take that cob out and make yoself free, Captain Montgomery—and ladies all. You Sal, you hussy, git up f'm thar this minit, and take some exercise! for the land's sake, ain't you got no sense at all?—settin' thar on that cold rock and you jes' ben married last night, and your pores all open!"

The ladies wanted to go aboard the boat, they bade the kind, hospitable old woman good by, and went away. But Captain Montgomery staid behind, because he knew how badly the old lady wanted to talk, and he was a good soul and loved to please her.

Ah, that was a good man was Captain Ed. Montgomery, and the moment I saw that paragraph about him the other day I remembered how kind it was of him to always stop and buy that old Arkansas woman's green wood and pay her the highest market price for it when he could no more burn it than he could burn an iceberg. It was so soggy, too, and wet, and heavy. I remember how, whenever he blew the whistle to land there, the mate used to sing out hoarsely and in bitterness of spirit, "Larboard watch—turn out! Stand by, men, to take in some ballast!" But you can rest assured I am not sorry old Captain Ed. Montgomery is alive and well yet.

FROM THE *Golden Era*, JAN. 28, 1866.

MYSTERIOUS NEWSPAPER MAN

[*In a letter to the* TERRITORIAL ENTERPRISE, *on the "Russian Telegraph Company," "Mark Twain" says:*]

COLONEL CONWAY has appointed "Brian McAllister," (Jerome), late of the New Orleans *Times*, on his staff, as his Secretary. The man is talented, and it is well to have a newspaper man on such an expedition—but then there is a graver consideration than this to be taken into account; there is matter for thought, for calculation, for careful weighing here; there is room for hesitation, for doubt, for profound misgivings here—WILL THE DRIED SALMON HOLD OUT? I would not wantonly interfere with the hopes and ambitious dreams of the newspaper creature; I would not wantonly crush him to the earth—but I put it on broad national, educational, humanitarian grounds, and ask: Is it well thus to jeopardize the success of so mighty an enterprise as this? The matter is worthy of the most serious consideration. This newspaper man will travel with the land party and transportation facilities will be extremely limited—the case would be very different if he were going with the fleet, because then an extra ship—. But I suppose I have made myself understood?

FROM THE *Golden Era*, FEB. 18, 1866.

BIOGRAPHICAL SKETCH OF GEORGE WASHINGTON

THIS DAY, MANY years ago precisely, George Washington was born. How full of significance the thought! Especially to those among us who have had a similar experience, though subsequently; and still more especially to the young, who should take him for a model and faithfully try to be like him, undeterred by the frequency with which the same thing has been attempted by American youths before them and not satisfactorily accomplished. George Washington was the youngest of nine children, eight of whom were the offspring of his uncle and his aunt. As a boy he gave no promise of the greatness he was one day to achieve. He was ignorant of the commonest accomplishments of youth. He could not even lie. But then he never had any of those precious advantages which are within the reach of the humblest of the boys of the present day. Any boy can lie, now. I could lie before I could stand—yet this sort of sprightliness was so common in our family that little notice was taken of it. Young George appears to have had no sagacity whatsoever. It is related of him that he once chopped down his father's favorite cherry tree, and then didn't know enough to keep dark about it. He came near going to sea, once, as a midshipman; but when his mother represented to him that he must necessarily be absent when he was away from home, and that this must continue to be the case until he got back, the sad truth struck him so forcibly that he ordered his trunk ashore, and quietly but firmly refused to serve in the navy and fight the battles of his king so long as the effect of it would be to discommode his mother. The great rule of his life was, that procrastination was the thief of time, and that we should always do unto others. This is the golden rule. Therefore, he would never discommode his mother.

Young George Washington was actuated in all things by the highest and purest principles of morality, justice and right. He was a model in every way worthy of the emulation of youth. Young George was always prompt and faithful in the discharge of every duty. It has been said of him, by the historian, that he was always on hand, like a thousand of brick. And well deserved was this compliment. The aggregate of the building material specified might have been largely increased—might have been doubled even—without doing full justice to these high qualities in the subject of this sketch. Indeed, it would hardly be possible to express in bricks the exceeding promptness and fidelity of young George Washington. His was a soul whose manifold excellencies were beyond the ken and computation of mathematics, and bricks are, at the least, but an inadequate vehicle for the conveyance of a comprehension of the moral sublimity of a nature so pure as his.

Young George W. was a surveyor in early life—a surveyor of an inland port—a sort of country surveyor; and under a commission from Gov. Dinwiddie, he set out to survey his way four hundred miles through a trackless forest, infested with Indians, to procure the liberation of some English prisoners. The historian says the Indians were the most depraved of their species, and did nothing but lay for white men, whom they killed for the sake of robbing them. Considering that white men only traveled through the country at the rate of one a year, they were probably unable to do what might be termed a land-office business in their line. They did not rob young G. W.; one savage made the attempt, but failed; he fired at the subject of this sketch from behind a tree, but the subject of this sketch immediately snaked him out from behind a tree and took him prisoner.

The long journey failed of success; the French would not give up the prisoners, and Wash went sadly back home again. A regiment was raised to go and make a rescue, and he took command of it. He caught the French out in the rain and tackled them with great intrepidity. He defeated them in ten minutes, and their commander handed in his checks. This was the battle of Great Meadows.

After this, a good while, George Washington became Commander in Chief of the American armies, and had an exceedingly dusty time of it all through the Revolution. But every now and then he turned a jack from the bottom and surprised the enemy. He kept up his lick for seven long years, and hazed the British from Harrisburg to Halifax—and America was free! He served two terms as President, and would have been President yet if he had lived—even so did the people honor the Father of his Country. Let the youth of America take his incomparable character for a model and try it one jolt, anyhow. Success is possible—let them remember that—success is possible, though there are chances against it.

I could continue this biography, with profit to the rising generation, but I shall have to drop the subject at present, because of other matters which must be attended to.

FROM THE *Golden Era*, MARCH 4, 1864.

BUSTED, AND GONE ABROAD

THE TERM—"Busted"—applies to most people here. When a noted speculator breaks, you all hear of it; but when Smith and Jones and

Brown go under, they make no stir; they are talked about among a small circle of gratified acquaintances, but they industriously keep up appearances, and the world at large go on thinking them as rich as ever. The lists of rich stock operators of two years ago have quietly sunk beneath the wave and financially gone to the devil. Smithers, who owned a hundred and ninety-six feet in one of the big mines, and gave such costly parties, has sent his family to Europe. Blivens, who owned so much in another big mine, and kept such fast horses, has sent his family to Germany, for their health, where they can sport a princely magnificence on fifty dollars a month. Bloggs, who was high-you-muck-a-muck of another great mine, has sent his family home to rusticate a while with his father-in-law. All the nabobs of '63 are pretty much ruined, but they send their families foraging in foreign climes, and hide their poverty under a show of "appearances." If a man's family start anywhere on the steamer now, the public say: "There's the death rattle again—another Croesus has gone in." These are sad, sad times. We are all "busted," and our families are exiled in foreign lands.

FROM THE *Golden Era*, JAN. 28, 1866.

A SAN FRANCISCO MILLIONAIRE

THEY TELL a story of M., a story which shows that once in his life, at any rate, he grew lavish and reckless, and squandered his money with a desperate prodigality.

He had loaned one S. (I cannot recollect his real name,) a thousand dollars or so, at about five per cent a month, and the man invested it in coal, expecting to make a profitable speculation out of it. But the price of coal took a downward track, and went falling, falling, falling, till it was not worth more than half the sum S. had borrowed of M.

M. took the place of S.'s shadow, and haunted him day and night. At last the ruined speculator could stand it no longer, and he sought the privacy of his own chamber and blew out his brains. He left M. a heavy loser, and M. abandoned himself to frightful dissipation for a single hour. He was worried by his loss and bothered by the accusation that he was the prime cause of poor S.'s death. He took several friends into a cellar and treated them to a glass of lager apiece. They talked a while, and then got up to leave. The barkeeper reminded them that the beer was not paid for yet. The guests moved up to the counter—each with his hand in his pocket, but M. advanced with a wild light in his eye and waved them impressively aside. He said: "No, I pays for all dis myself! Vot I cares for anydings now? My friend is dead, shentlemen—my friend vot I lofed. Poor S., he's plode his prains out, and didn't pay me. Vot I cares for anydings now? I lif, now, after dis, shentlemen—I lif gay und spends my money—I safes no money to loan to people vot go und kill himself before he pay. No, I pays for dis peer myself—I vill be gay und regulus—dam de expensus!"

But that one fearful orgie was his first and his last. The reflections of a cooler moment showed him that the "expensus" were worthy of graver consideration.

FROM THE *Golden Era*, FEB. 25, 1866.

MISERIES OF WASHOE MEN

THOSE OF YOU who owe the Russ House for board and expect to save yourselves trouble when you come here by stopping at the Occidental, look out; Mr. Hardenburgh, formerly of the Russ, is in the office of the

Occidental now. And you who owe the Cosmopolitan and propose to stop at the Occidental, beware! for Mr. Smith, formerly of the Cosmopolitan, is in the Occidental office now. And you who owe the Occidental and think to shirk calamity by patronizing the Cosmopolitan, go slow! for Mr. Olmstead and Mr. Childs clerk at the latter hotel now, instead of the former. You had better all come down to your work and go and hang out at the Miners' Restaurant. They have gone and changed things around so now that there is no show for me anywhere. I want to keep my friends out of trouble, though, and so I sound the above note of warning. Amiraux was here from Carson the other day, but he would not stay because his feelings were hurt. He said: "I went to the What Cheer, and I found a fellow from the Brooklyn there; and I went to the Occidental, and I found a fellow from the Russ there; and then I went to the Cosmopolitan, and if there was one clerk there from the Occidental there was a thousand. I am not going to stay in this place—you hear *me!* Damn such a town."

FROM THE *Golden Era*, JAN. 28, 1866.

NEW YEAR'S DAY

THERE WAS A GOOD deal of visiting done here on New Year's Day. The the air was balmy and spring-like, and the day was in every way suited to that sort of business. I say business, because it is more like business than pleasure when you call at a house where all are strangers, and the majority of one's New Year's Calls are necessarily of that description. You soon run through the list of your personal friends—and that part of the day's performances affords you genuine satisfaction—and then Smith comes along and puts you through your paces before a hundred people who treat you kindly, but whom you dare not joke with. You can be as easy and comfortable as a mud-turtle astraddle of a sawyer, but you must observe some show of decorum—you must behave yourself. It is irksome to me to behave myself. Therefore, I had rather call on people who know me and will kindly leave me entirely unrestrained, and simply employ themselves in looking out for the spoons.

When I started out visiting, at noon, the atmosphere was laden with a sweet perfume—a grateful incense that told of flowers, and green fields, and breezy forests far away. But this was only soda-water sentiment, for I soon discovered that these were the odors of the barbershop, and came from the heads of small squads of carefully-dressed young men who were out paying their annual calls.

I took wine at one house and some fruit at another, and after that I began to yearn for some breakfast. It took me two hours to get it. A lady had just given me the freedom of her table when a crowd of gentlemen arrived and my sense of propriety compelled me to destroy nothing more than a cup of excellent coffee. At the next house I got no further than coffee again, being similarly interrupted; at the next point of attack there were too many strange young ladies present, and at the next and the next, something always happened to interfere with my arrangements. I do not know, but perhaps it would be better to defer one's New Year's calls until after breakfast. I did finally corral that meal, and in the house of a stranger—a stranger, too, who was so pleasant that I was almost tempted to create a famine in her house.

It used to be customary for people to drink too much in the course of their annual visits, but few offended in this way on this occasion. I saw one well-dressed gentleman sitting on the curb-stone, propping his face between his knees, and clasping his shins with his hands; but he was the only caller I saw so much discouraged during the whole day. He said he had started out most too early, and I suppose he was right. Wisdom teaches us that none but birds should go out early, and that not even birds should do it unless they are out of worms. Some of the ladies dressed "in character" on New Year's. I found Faith, Hope and Charity in one house, dealing out claret punch and kisses to the annual pilgrims. They had two kinds of kisses—those which you bite and "chaw" and swallow, and those which you simply taste, and then lick your chops and feel streaky. The only defect there was in the arrangement was that you were not permitted to take your choice. Two other ladies personated Mary, Queen of Scots, and Queen Elizabeth; I also found a Cleopatra and a Hebe and a Semiramis and a Maria Antoinette;

also a Beauty and the Beast. A young lady, formerly of Carson, was the Beauty, and took the character well; and I suppose Beecher was the Beast, but he was not calculated for the part. I think those are very neat compliments for both parties.

When it came to visiting among strangers, at last, I soon grew tired and quit. You enter with your friend and are introduced formally to some formal looking ladies. You bow painfully and wish the party a happy New Year. You then learn that the party desire that a like good fortune may fall to your lot. You are invited to sit down, and you do so. About this time the door-bell rings, and Jones, Brown and Murphy bluster in and bring the familiar fragrance of the barber shop with them. They are acquainted. They inquire cordially after the absent members of the family and the distant relatives of the same, and relate laughable adventures of the morning that haven't got anything funny about them. Then they cast up accounts and determine how many calls they have made and how many they have got to inflict yet. The ladies respond by exhibiting a balance sheet of their own New Year's Day transactions. Yourself and your friend are then conducted with funeral solemnity into the back parlor, where you sip some wine with imposing ceremony. If your human instincts get the upper hand of you and you explode a joke, an awful sensation creeps over you such as a man experiences when he catches himself whistling at a funeral. It is time for you to go, then.

New Year's was pretty generally enjoyed here, up stairs and down. At one place where I called, a servant girl was needed, for something, and the bell was rung for her several times without effect. Madame went below to see what the matter was, and found Bridget keeping "open house" and entertaining thirteen muscular callers in one batch. Up stairs there had been only eleven calls received, all told. One chambermaid notified her mistress that extra help must be procured for New Year's Day, as she and the cook had made arrangements to keep open house in the kitchen, and they desired that their visitors should not be discommoded by interruptions emanating from above stairs. I am told that nearly all the Biddies in town kept open house. Some of them set finer tables than their mistresses. The reason was because the latter did not consider anything more than tea and coffee and cakes necessary for their tables (being church members) but the formed seized upon wines, brandies and all the hidden luxuries the closets afforded. Some people affect to think servant girls won't take liberties with people's things, but I suppose it is a mistake.

FROM THE *Golden Era*, JAN. 14, 1866. [T. E.]

ON BOOT-BLACKS

THE BOOT-BLACKING facilities of Sacramento are unsurpassed by those of any city in the world I should judge. There is a boot-blacking stand in front of every saloon—which is to say, there are boot-blacking stands all along. All these prominent localities which, in other cities, are usually sacred to the peanut interest, are here seized upon and held by the boot-black. These mute facts tell the stranger that Sacramento, which is now so irreproachably cleanly, has long and fearful attacks of alternate mud and dust. In further evidence of this, I remarked that out of the one hundred and eighty-four gentlemen who lounged about the front of the Orleans Hotel when I came down and asked for breakfast at ten minutes past 12 o'clock to-day and didn't get any, a hundred and seventy had their boots blacked. The other fourteen were undergoing the boot-blacking operation in chairs backed up against the neighboring walls. Now there was not a particle of dust in the air, and no mud under foot; and nothing but inveterate habit could have made these people all go and get their boots blacked with such singular unanimity, when there was no real necessity for it. I never saw a place before where everybody, without exception, had their boot blacked. Every time I noticed, to-day, that my boots were attracting attention, I went and got them blacked. And I learned something. I learned that a Chinaman has no talent for blacking boots, and makes a miserable job of it. When you desire the services of a real artist, always choose one of the three naturally gifted species of boot-blacks—a freedman, or a colored citizen, or a nigger. They understand the business.

FROM THE *Golden Era*, MARCH 11, 1866.

REFLECTIONS ON THE SABBATH

The day of rest comes but once a week, and sorry I am that it does not come oftener. Man is so constituted that he can stand more rest than this. I often think regretfully that it would have been so easy to have two Sundays in a week, and yet it was not so ordained. The omnipotent Creator could have made the world in three days just as easily as he made it in six, and this would have doubled the Sundays. Still it is not our place to criticise the wisdom of the Creator. When we feel a depraved inclination to question the judgment of Providence in stacking up double eagles in the coffers of Michael Reese and leaving better men to dig for a livelihood, we ought to stop and consider that we are not expected to help order things, and so drop the subject. If all-powerful Providence grew weary after six days' labor, such worms as we are might reasonably expect to break down in three, and so require two Sundays—but as I said before, it ill becomes us to hunt up flaws in matters which are so far out of our jurisdiction. I hold that no man can meddle with the exclusive affairs of Providence and offer suggestions for their improvement, without making himself in a manner conspicious. Let us take things as we find them—though, I am free to confess, it goes against the grain to do it, sometimes.

What put me into this religious train of mind, was attending church at Dr. Wadsworth's this morning. I had not been to church before for many months, because I never could get a pew, and therefore had to sit in the gallery among the sinners. I stopped that because my proper place was down among the elect, inasmuch as I was brought up a Presbyterian, and consider myself a brevet member of Dr. Wadsworth's church. I always was a brevet. I was sprinkled in infancy, and look upon that as conferring the rank of Brevet Presbyterian. It affords none of the emoluments of the Regular Church—simply confers honorable rank upon the recipient and the right to be punished as a Presbyterian hereafter; that is, the substantial Presbyterian punishment of fire and brimstone instead of this heterodox hell of remorse of conscience of these blamed wildcat religions. The heaven and hell of the wildcat religions are vague and ill defined but there is nothing mixed about the Presbyterian heaven and hell. The Presbyterian hell is all misery; the heaven all happiness—nothing to do. But when a man dies on a wildcat basis, he will never rightly know hereafter which department he is in—but he will think he is in hell anyhow, no matter which place he goes to; because in the good place they pro-gress, pro-gress, pro-gress—study, study, study, all the time—and if this isn't hell I don't know what is; and in the bad place he will be worried by remorse of conscience. Their bad place is preferable, though, because eternity is long, and before a man got half through it he would forget what it was he had been so sorry about. Naturally he would then become cheerful again; but the party who went to heaven would go on progressing and progressing, and studying and studying until he would finally get discouraged and wish he were in hell, where he wouldn't require such a splendid education.

Dr. Wadsworth never fails to preach an able sermon; but every now and then, with an admirable assumption of not being aware of it, he will get off a firstrate joke and then frown severely at any one who is surprised into smiling at it. This is not fair. It is like throwing a bone to a dog and then arresting him with a look just as he is going to seize it. Several people there on Sunday suddenly laughed and as suddenly stopped again, when he gravely gave the Sunday school books a blast and spoke of "the good little boys in them who always went to Heaven, and the bad little boys who infallibly got drowned on Sunday," and then swept a savage frown around the house and blighted every smile in the congregation.

FROM THE *Golden Era*, MARCH 18, 1866.

V. MARK TWAIN INVESTIGATES SPIRITUALISM

Mark Twain
INVESTIGATES SPIRITUALISM

MODERN SPIRITUALISM, *inaugurated when the Fox sisters heard mysterious rappings in Rochester late in the forties, spread rapidly throughout the United States and England. Estimates place the number of American spiritualists during the fifties as high as two million. Recantations brought reaction during the following decade; only in California did spiritualism continue to hold its own during the Civil War. Mrs. Emma Harding Britten in her history of spiritualism maintains that her cult thrived on the Pacific Slope for three reasons: the wonderful transparency of the atmosphere encouraged spiritual phenomena, the heavy charges of mineral magnetism from the gold deposits set up favorable currents, and the notably strong passions of the forty-niners tended to create "unusual magnetic emanations." On the other hand, skeptics have suggested that a strong taste for gambling and the disappointments of mining and frontier life were largely responsible for the popularity of such activities as astrology and spiritualism. Not entirely unexpected, then, are the stories of the disappointed Mexican grandee, General Vallejo, delighting in the twanging of a spirit guitar, of James Marshall, discoverer of gold, putting all of his faith in spirit guidance, or of Peter O'Riley, co-discoverer of the Comstock, going insane after following the advice of a spirit to use his fortune to sink a shaft in a barren hill near Genoa.*

Spiritualistic activities during Mark Twain's stay in San Francisco centered around the lectures and seances of two very successful mediums, Ada Hoyt Foye and Laura Cuppy. Mrs. Foye, young, auburn-haired, and good-looking, held public seances once a week in which she demonstrated her ability as a "rapping and test medium." Dark-haired, midde-aged, dumpy Mrs. Cuppy, on the other hand, drew her audiences by mixing spiritualism and pleas for a single standard for men and women. Her society, calling itself the Friends of Progress, divided its interest between communication with the dead and discussion of edifying topics such as "Woman—her End—her Aim." While the curious thronged to the meetings, the opponents, led by the BULLETIN, attacked Foye and Cuppy, accusing them of being immoral and dangerous influences in the community. Within the space of a month the BULLETIN reported three cases of insanity arising from undue exposure to spiritualism; one of the victims, the G. C. DeMerrit mentioned by Mark Twain, went beserk while attending a Friends of Progress meeting.

It was inevitable that Mark Twain, with his curiosity about such movements, should investigate spiritualism. He started his campaign by burlesquing a story, then going the rounds among the believers, about a servant girl being mauled by a spirit. A week later he attended Ada Foye's meeting and asked questions; the following week he was a member of the committee that sat on the stage and watched for monkey business. In his reports, when he was serious, he neither scoffed nor believed, but he was quick to point out that he found no more fanaticism among members of this "wild cat religion" than he had seen among earnest Presbyterians. Except for using the device to introduce an article on the signal corps and to make some jibes at the Board of Supervisors, he adhered in his discussions strictly to the subject of spiritualism. Charles Warren Stoddard, who accompanied him to at least one seance, was tempted for a moment to follow Laura Cuppy. Prentice Mulford, a fellow journalist, succumbed whole-heartedly, devoting most of his later writings to presenting his own brand of spiritualism. When Mark Twain left San Francisco he was still a skeptic.

THE KEARNY STREET GHOST STORY

DISEMBODIED SPIRITS have been on the rampage now for more than a month past in the house of one Albert Krum, in Kearny street—so much so that the family find it impossible to keep a servant forty-eight hours. The moment a new and unsuspecting servant-maid gets fairly to bed and her light blown out, one of those dead and damned scalliwags takes her by the hair and just "hazes" her; grabs her by the waterfall and snakes her out of bed and bounces her on the floor two or three times; other disorderly corpses shy old boots at her head, and bootjacks, and brittle chamber furniture—washbowls, pitchers, hair-oil, teeth-brushes, hoop-skirts—anything that comes handy those phantoms seize and hurl at Bridget, and pay no more attention to her howling than if it were music. The spirits tramp, tramp, tramp, about the house at dead of night, and when a light is struck the footsteps cease and the promenader is not visible, and just as soon as the light is out that dead man goes waltzing around again. They are a bloody lot. The young lady of the house was lying in bed one night with the gas turned down low, when a figure approached her through the gloom, whose ghastly aspect and solemn carriage chilled her to the heart. What do you suppose she did?—jumped up and seized the intruder?—threw a slipper at him?—"laid" him with a misquotation from Scripture? No—none of these. But with admirable presence of mind she covered up her head and yelled. That is what she did. Few young women would have thought of doing that. The ghost came and stood by the bed and groaned—a deep, agonizing, heart-broken groan—and laid a bloody kitten on the pillow by the girl's head. And then it groaned again, and sighed, "Oh, God, and must it be?" and bet another bloody kitten. It groaned a third time in sorrow and tribulation, and went one kitten better. And thus the sorrowing spirit stood there, moaning in its anguish and unloading its mewing cargo, until it had stacked up a whole litter of nine little bloody kittens on the girl's pillow, and then, still moaning, moved away and vanished.

When lights were brought, there were the kittens, with the finger-marks of bloody hands upon their white fur—and the old mother cat, that had come after them, swelled her tail in mortal fear and refused to take hold of them. What do you think of that? what would you think of a ghost that came to your bedside at dead of night and had kittens?

FROM THE *Golden Era*, JAN. 28, 1866. [T. E.]

AMONG THE SPIRITS

THERE WAS AN AUDIENCE of about 400 ladies and gentlemen present, and plenty of newspaper people—neuters. I saw a good-looking, earnest-faced, pale-red-haired, neatly dressed, young woman standing on a little stage behind a small deal table with slender legs and no drawers—the table, understand me; I am writing in a hurry, but I do not desire to confound my description of the table with my description of the lady. The lady was Mrs. Foye.

As I was coming up town with the *Examiner* reporter, in the early part of the evening, he said he had seen a gambler named Gus Graham shot down in a town in Illinois years ago, by a mob, and as probably he was the only person in San Francisco who knew of the circumstance, he thought he would "give the spirits Graham to chaw on awhile." [N. B. This young creature is a Democrat, and speaks with the native strength and inelegance of his tribe.] In the course of the show he wrote his old pal's name on a slip of paper and folded it up tightly and put in a hat which was passed around, and which already had about five hundred similar documents in it. The pile was dumped on the table and the medium began to take them up one by one and lay them aside, asking: "Is this spirit present?—or this?—or this?" About one in fifty would rap, and the person who sent up the name would rise in his place and question the defunct. At last a spirit seized the medium's hand and wrote "Gus Graham" backwards. Then the medium went skirmishing through the papers for the corresponding name. And that old sport knew his card by the back! When the medium came to it, after picking up fifty others, he rapped! A committee-man unfolded the paper and it was the right one. I sent for it and got it. It was all right.

However, I suppose "all them Democrats" are on sociable terms with the devil. The young man got up and asked:

"Did you die in '51?—'52?—'53?—'54?—"

Ghost—"Rap, rap, rap."

"Did you die of cholera?—diarrhea?—dysentery?—dog-bite?—small-pox?—violent death?—"

"Rap, rap, rap."

"Were you hanged?—drowned?—stabbed?—shot?—"

"Rap, rap, rap."

"Did you die in Mississippi?—Kentucky?—New York?—Sandwich Islands?—Texas?—Illinois?—"

"Rap, rap, rap."

"In Adams county?—Madison?—Randolph ?—"

"Rap, rap, rap."

It was no use trying to catch the departed gambler. He knew his hand and played it like a Major.

I was surprised. I had a very dear friend, who, I had heard, had gone to the spirit land, or perdition, or some of those places, and I desired to know something concerning him. There were something concerning him. There was something so awful, though, about talking with living, sinful lips to the ghostly dead, that I could hardly bring myself to rise and speak. But at last I got tremblingly up and said with low and reverent voice:

"Is the spirit of John Smith present?"

"Whack! whack! whack! whack!"

God bless me. I believe all the dead and damned John Smiths between hell and San Francisco tackled that poor little table at once! I was considerably set back—stunned, I may say. The audience urged me to go on, however, and I said:

"What did you die of?"

The Smiths answered to every disease and casualty that man can die of.

"Where did you die!"

They answered yes to every locality I could name while my geography held out.

"Are you happy where you are?"

There was a vigorous and unanimous "No!" from the late Smiths.

"Is it warm there?"

An educated Smith seized the medium's hand and wrote:

"It's no name for it."

"Did you leave any Smiths in that place when you came away?"

"Dead loads of them."

I fancied, I heard the shadowy Smiths chuckle at this feeble joke—the rare joke that there could be live load of Smiths where all are dead.

"How many Smiths are present?"

"Eighteen millions—the procession now reaches from here to the other side of China."

"Then there are many Smiths in the kingdom of the lost?"

"The Prince Apollyon calls all newcomers Smith on general principles; and continues to do so until he is corrected, if he chances to be mistaken."

"What do lost spirits call their dread abode?"

"They call it the Smithsonian Institute."

I got hold of the right Smith at last—the particular Smith I was after—my dear, lost, lamented friend—and learned that he died a violent death. I feared as much. He said his wife talked him to death. Poor wretch!

But without any nonsense, Mrs. Foye's seance was a very astonishing affair to me—and a very entertaining one. The *Examiner* man's "old pard," the gambler, was too many for me. He answered every question exactly right; and his disembodied spirit, invisible to mortal eyes, must have been prowling around that hall last night. That is, unless this pretended spiritualism is only that other black art called clairvoyance, after all. And yet, the clairvoyant can only tell what is in your mind—but once or twice last night the spirits brought facts to the minds of their questioners which the latter had forgotten before. Well, I cannot make anything out of it. I asked the *Examiner* man what he thought of it, and he said, in the Democratic dialect: "Well, I don't know—I don't know—but it's d——d funny." He did not mean that it was laughable—he only meant that it was perplexing. But such is the language of Democracy.

FROM THE *Golden Era*, FEB. 4, 1866. [T. E.]

MARK TWAIN A COMMITTEE MAN

AFTER THE HOUSE was crowded with ladies and gentlemen, Mrs. Foye stepped out upon the stage and said it was usual to elect a committee of two gentlemen to sit up there and see that everything was conducted with perfect honesty and fairness. She said she wished the audience to name gentlemen whose integrity, whose conscientiousness—in a word whose high moral character, in every respect, was notorious in the community. The majority of the audience arose with one impulse and called my name. This handsome compliment was as grateful as it was graceful, and I felt the tears spring to my eyes. I trust I shall never do anything to forfeit the generous confidence San Francisco has thus shown in me. This touching compliment is none the less grateful to me when I reflect that it took me two days to get to it up. I "put up" that hand myself. I got all my friends to promise to go there and vote for me to be on that committee—and having reported a good deal in Legislatures, I knew how to do it right. I had a two-third vote secured—I wanted enough to elect me over the medium's veto, you know. I was elected, and I was glad of it. I thought I would feel a good deal better satisfied if I could have a chance to examine into this mystery myself, without being obliged to take somebody else's word for its fairness, and I did not go on that stand to find fault or make fun of the affair—a thing which would not speak well for my modesty when I reflect that so many men so much older and wiser than I am see nothing in Spiritualism to scoff at, but firmly believe in it as a religion.

Mr. Whiting was chosen as the other committeeman, and we sat down at a little table on the stage with the medium, and proceeded to business. We wrote the names of various departed persons. Mr. W.

wrote a good many, but I found that I did not know many dead people; however, I put in the names of two or three whom I had known well, and then filled out the list with names of citizens of San Francisco who had been distinguished in life, so that most persons in the audience could tell whether facts stated by such spirits concerning themselves were correct or not. I will remark here that not a solitary spirit summoned by me paid the least attention to the invitation. I never got a word out of any of them. One of Mr. Whiting's spirits came up and stated some things about itself which were correct. Then some five hundred closely folded slips of paper containing names, were dumped in a pile on the table, and the lady began to lay them aside one by one. Finally a rap was heard. I took the folded paper; the spirit, so-called, seized the lady's hand and wrote "J. M. Cooke" backwards and upside down on a sheet of paper. I opened the slip I held, and, as Captain Cuttle would say, "J. M. Cooke" was the "dientical" name in it. A gentleman in the audience said he sent up the name. He asked a question or so, and then the spirit wrote "Would like to communicate with you alone." The privacy of this ghost was respected, and he was permitted to go to thunder again unmolested. "William Nelson" reported himself from the other world, and in answer to questions asked by a former friend of his in the audience, said he was aged 24 when he died; died by violence; died in a battle; was a soldier; had fought both in the infantry and cavalry; fell at Chickamauga: had been a Catholic on earth—was not one now. Then in answer to a pelting volley of questions, the shadowy warrior wrote: "I don't want to answer any more about it." Exit Nelson.

About this time it was suggested that a couple of Germans be added to the committee, and it was done. Mr. Wallenstein, an elderly man, came forward, and also Mr. Ollendorf, a spry young fellow, cocked and primed for a sensation. They wrote some names. Then young Ollendorf said something which sounded like:

"Ist ein geist hierans?" [bursts of laughter from the audience.]

Three raps—signifying that there was a geist hierans.

"Vollen sie schriehen? [more laughter.] Three raps.

"Finzig stollen, linsowftterowlickter-hairowfterfrowleinerubackfolderol?" [Oh, this is too rough, you know. I can't keep the run of this sort of thing.] Incredible as it may seem, the spirit cheerfully answered yes to that astonishing proposition.

Young Ollendorf sprang to his feet in a state of consuming excitement. He exclaimed:

"Laties and shentlemen ! I write de name for a man vot lifs! Speerit rabbing dells me he ties in yahr eighteen hoondert und dwelf, but he yoos as live und helty as—"

The Medium—"Sit down, sir!"

Mr. O.—"But de speerit cheat!—dere is no such speerit—" [All this time applause and laughter by turns from the audience.]

Medium—Take your seat, sir, and I will explain this matter."

And she explained. And in that explanation she left off a blast which was so terrific that I half expected to see young Ollendorf shoot up through the roof. She said he had come up there with fraud and deceit and cheating in his heart, and a kindred spirit had come from the land of shadows to commune with him! She was terribly bitter. She said in substance, though not in words, that perdition was full of just such fellows as Ollendorf, and they were ready on the slightest pretext to rush in and assume anybody's name, and rap, and write, and lie, and swindle with a perfect looseness whenever they could rope in a living affinity like poor Ollendorf to communicate with! [Great applause and laughter.]

Ollendorf stood his ground with good pluck, and was going to open his batteries again, when a storm of cries arose all over the house. "Get down! Go on! Clear out! Speak on—we'll hear you! Climb down from that platform! Stay where you are—Vamose! Stick to your post—say your say!"

The medium rose up and said if Ollendorf remained, she would not. She recognized no one's right to come there and insult her by practicing a deception upon her and attempting to bring ridicule upon so solemn a thing as her religious belief.

The audience then became quiet, and the subjugated Ollendorf retired from the platform.

The other German raised a spirit, questioned it at some length in his own language, and said the answers were correct. The medium claims to be entirely unacquainted with the German language.

A spirit seized the medium's hand and wrote "G. L. Smith" very distinctly. She hunted through the mass of papers, and finally the spirit rapped. She handed me the folded paper she had just picked up. It had "T. J. Smith" in it. [You never can depend on these Smiths; you call for one and the whole tribe will come clattering out of hell to answer you.] Upon further inquiry it was discovered that both these Smiths were present. We chose "T. J." A gentleman in the audience said that was his Smith. So he questioned him, and Smith said he died by violence; he had been a teacher; not a school-teacher, but (after some hesitation) a teacher of religion, and was a sort of a cross between a Universalist and a Unitarian; has got straightened out and changed his opinion since he left here; said he was perfectly happy. Mr. George Purnell, having been added to the committee, proceeded in connection with myself, Mrs. Foye and a number of persons in the audience, to question this talkative and frolicksome old parson. Among spirits, I judge he is the gayest of the gay. He said he had no tangible body; a bullet could pass through him and never make a hole; rain could pass through him as through vapor, and not discommode him in the least (wherefore I suppose he don't know enough to come in when it rains—or don't care enough); says heaven and hell are simply mental conditions—spirits in the former have happy and contented minds; and those in the latter are torn by remorse of conscience; says as far as he is concerned, he is all right—he is happy; would not say whether he was a very good or a very bad man on earth (the shrewd old water-proof nonentity!—I asked the question so that I might average my own chances for his luck in the other world, but he saw my drift); says he has an occupation there—puts in his time teaching and being taught; says there are spheres—grades of perfection—he is making pretty good progress—has been promoted a sphere or so since his matriculation; (I said mentally: "Go slow, old man, go slow—you have got all eternity before you"—and he replied not); he don't know how many spheres there are (but I suppose there must be millions, because if a man goes galloping through them at the rate this old Universalist is doing, he will get through an infinitude of them by the time he has been there as long as old Sesostris and those ancient mummies; and there is no estimating how high he will get in even the infancy of eternity—I am afraid the old man is scouring along rather too fast for the style of his surroundings, and the length of time he has got on his hands); says spirits cannot feel heat or cold (which militates somewhat against all my notions of orthodox damnation—fire and brimstone); says spirits commune with each other by thought—they have no language; says the distinctions of the sex are preserved there—and so forth and so on.

The old parson wrote and talked for an hour, and showed by his quick, shrewd, intelligent replies, that he had not been sitting up nights in the other world for nothing, he had been prying into everything worth knowing, and finding out everything he possibly could—as he said himself, when he did not understand a thing he hunted up a spirit who could explain it; consequently he is pretty thoroughly posted; and for his accommodating conduct and its uniform courtesy to me, I sincerely hope he will continue to progress at his present velocity until he lands on the very roof of the highest sphere of all, and thus achieves perfection.

I have made a report of those proceedings which every person present will say is correct in every particular. But I do not know any more about the queer mystery than I did before. I could not even tell where the knocks were made, though they were not two feet from me. Sometimes they seemed to be on the corner of the table, sometimes under the center of it, and sometimes they seemed to proceed from the medium's knee joints. I could not locate them at all, though; they only had a general seeming of being in any one spot; sometimes they even seemed to be in the air. As to where that remarkable intelligence emanates from which directs those strangely accurate replies, that is beyond my reason. I cannot any more account for that than I could explain those wonderful miracles performed by Hindoo jugglers. I cannot tell whether the power is supernatural in either case or not, and I never expect to know as long as I live. It is necessarily impossible to *know*—and it is mighty hard to fully believe what you *don't* know.

But I am going to see it through, now, if I do not go crazy—an eccentricity that seems singularly apt to follow investigations of spiritualism.

FROM THE *Golden Era*, FEB. 11, 1865. [T.E.]

SPIRITUAL INSANITY

I (TOGETHER WITH THE *Bulletin*) have watched, with deep concern, the distress being wrought in our midst by spiritualism, during the past week or two; I (like the *Bulletin*) have done all I could to crush out the destroyer; I have published full reports of the seances of the so-called "Friends of Progress," and the *Bulletin* has left out three columns of printed paragraphs pasted together by its New York correspondent to make room for a report of the spiritualist Laura Cuppy's lecture; and I have followed in the *Bulletin's* wake and shouted every few days, "Another Victim of the Wretched Delusion called Spiritualism!" and like that paper, have stated the number of persons it took to hold him and where his mother resided.

In some instances which have come under my notice, these symptoms are peculiarly sad. How touching it was, on Monday evening, in the Board of Supervisors—a body which should be a concentration of the wisdom and intellect of the city—to see Supervisor McCoppin, bereft of his accustomed sprightliness, and subdued, subjugated by spiritualism, rise in his place, and with bowed head, and stooping body, and frightened eyes peering from under overhanging brows, ejaculate in sepulchral tones:

"FEE—FAW—FUM!"

Great Heavens! to hear him say that and then sit down with the air of a man who has settled a mooted question forever, and done the work in a solid, substantial manner.

And it touched me to the very heart to see the Mayor of the city—a man of commanding presence and solemn demeanor—get up and repeat the following, as if it were a part of a litany:

Three blind mice,
See—how they—run.
The farmer's wife,
She cut off their tails
With the carving knife,
See—how—they run."

He then sat down and leaned his face in his hands, and Dr. Rowell got up and said:

"Spiritual department—paid spiritual department, when I was a Republican I poisoned rebels—now I am a Democrat, I poison Republicans. Woe, woe, woe, unto the traducers of the new light! woe, woe, woe, to the enemies of the new light! woe, woe, woe, unto them that hear the Cuppy and the Foye and the ministering spirits that fan us with invisible wings as they sweep by, and whisper eternal truths in our ears—woe, woe, woe!"

"Woe-haw, woe-haw, woe-haw-Buck, You *Duke!*" said Mr. Ashbury, impressively.

Mr. McCoppin (counting on his fingers)—One ery—o'ery—ickery—Ann; fillisy, fallallacy, Nicholas John; queevy, quavy, English navy—stinklum, stanklum, Buck. Alas, my poor, poor country."

Mr. Shrader said, with deep feeling, but without gesticulation or straining after effect:

"Let dogs delight to bark and bite,
For 'tis their nature thus—
Your little hands were never made
To tear out each other's eyes with."

My eyes filled with tears to see this body of really able men driveling in this foolish way, and as I walked sadly out, I said: "This is more spiritualism; the *Bulletin* and I will soon have to record the departure of the Board of Supervisors for Stockton. Poor creatures—to have kept out of the asylum on one pretext or another so long, and then to fall at last through so weak a thing as spiritualism."

FROM THE *Golden Era*, FEB. 18, 1866. [T.E.]

THE SIGNAL CORPS

I SAW SOMETHING the other night which surprised me more than my late investigations of spiritualism. It was some examples of the methods by the United States Signal Corps to telegraph information from point to point on the battle-fields of the rebellion. The Signal Corps "mediums" were Colonel Wicker, of the Russian Telegraph Expedition, and Mr. Jerome, Secretary of Mr. Conway of the same, both of whom were distinguished officers of Signal Corps throughout the war. Besides these two gentlemen there are only two other members of the corps on the coast.

In the late war a signal party was always stationed on the highest available point on the battle-field, and by waving flags they could telegraph any desired messages, word for word, to other signal stations ten miles off. At night, when torches were used, these messages have been read forty miles away, with a powerful glass. The flag, or torch, is waved right, left, up and down, and each movement represents a letter of the alphabet, I suppose, inasmuch as any villainous combination of letters and syllables you can get up can be readily telegraphed in this way with a good deal of expedition. These gentlemen I speak of sent messages the other night with walking-sticks, with their hands, their fingers, their eyes and even their moustaches! It is a little too deep for me.

One sat on one side of a large room, and the other at the opposite side. I wrote a long sentence and gave it to Jerome—he made a few rapid passes with his right arm like a crazy orchestra leader, and Colonel Wicker called off the sentence word for word. I confess that I suspected there was collusion there. So I whispered my next telegram to Jerome—the passes were made as before, and Colonel Wicker read them without a balk. I selected from a book a sentence which was full of uncommon and unpronounceable foreign words, pointed it out to Colonel Wicker, and he telegraphed it across to Jerome without a blunder. Then I gave Jerome another telegram; he placed two fingers on his knees and raised up one and then the other for a while, and the Colonel read the message. I furnished the latter with the following written telegram:

"General Jackson was wounded at first fire."

He went through with a series of elaborate winks with his eyes, and that other signal-sharp repeated the sentence correctly. I wrote:

"Thirteen additional cases of cholera reported this morning."

The accomplished Colonel telegraphed it to his confederate by simply stroking his moustache. There must be a horrible imposition about this thing somewhere, but I cannot get at it. They say that when they are in lecture rooms and parlors whence they are not close enough to speak to each other, they telegraph their comment on the company with their fingers, on their moustaches, or by gently refreshing themselves with a fan.

The signal Corps was one of the most important arms of the military service in the late war. It saved many a battle to the Union that must otherwise have been lost. Yet many of the officers of the army did not believe in its efficiency, regarded it as an ornamental innovation, and bore it strong ill-will. At the battle of Winchester, the officer in command after General Shields was wounded, had pressing need of reinforcements. The reserve were in full view six miles away. The Acting General asked a signal officer if he could order up a brigade. He said he could. "Then do it," said the General; "but," said he, "to make everything sure, I will dispatch an orderly for the reinforcements." The signal officer set his flags waving, and telegraphed: "Send up a brigade on the double-quick." Before the orderly was a hundred yards off, the anxious General gazing through his field glass, saw a brigade wheel into the plain, peel their coats and knapsacks off and throw them down, and come sweeping across on the double-quick. "By G——. here they come!—send back the orderly," said the General—"but I didn't think it could be done." FROM THE *Golden Era*, FEB. 18, 1866. [T.E.]..

THE NEW WILDCAT RELIGION

ANOTHER SPIRITUAL INVESTIGATOR—G. C. DeMerritt—passed his examination today, after a faithful attendance on the seances of the Friends of Progress, and was shipped, a raving maniac, to the insane asylum at Stockton—an institution which is getting to be quite a College of Progress.

People grow exasperated over these frequently occurring announcements of madness occasioned by fighting the tiger of spiritualism, and I think it is not fair. They abuse the spiritualists unsparingly, but I can remember when Methodist camp meetings and Campbellite revivals used to stock the asylums with religious lunatics, and yet the public kept their temper and said never a word. We don't cut up when madmen are bred by the old legitimate regular stock religions, but we can't allow wildcat religions to indulge in such disastrous experiments. I do not really own in the old regular stock, but I lean strongly toward it, and I naturally feel some little prejudice against all wildcat religions—still, I protest that it is not fair to excuse the one and abuse the other for the self-same rascality. I do not love the wildcat, but at the same time I do not like to see the wildcat imposed on merely because it is friendless. I know a great many spiritualists—good and worthy persons who sincerely and devotedly love their wildcat religion (but not regarding it as wildcat themselves, though, of course,)—and I know them to be persons in every way worthy of respect. They are men of business habits and good sense.

Now when I see such men as these, quietly but boldly come forward and consent to be pointed at as supporters of a wildcat religion, I almost feel as if it were presumptuous in some of us to assert without qualification that spiritualism *is* wildcat. And when I see these same persons cherishing, and taking to their honest bosoms and fondling this wildcat, with genuine affection and confidence, I feel like saying, "Well, if this is a wildcat religion, it pans out wonderfully like the old regular, after all." No—it goes against the grain; but still, loyalty to my Presbyterian bringing-up compels me to stick to the Presbyterian decision that spiritualism is neither more nor less than wildcat.

I do not take any credit to my better-balanced head because I never went crazy on Presbyterianism. We go too slow for that. You never see us ranting and shouting and tearing up the ground. You never heard of a Presbyterian going crazy on religion. Notice us, and you will see how we do. We get up of a Sunday morning and put on the best harness we have got and trip cheerfully down town; we subside into solemnity and enter the church; we stand up and duck our heads and bear down on a hymn book propped on the pew in front when the minister prays; we stand up again while our hired choir are singing, and look in the hymn book and check off the verses to see that they don't shirk any of the stanzas; we sit silent and grave while the minister is preaching, and count the waterfalls and bonnets furtively, and catch flies; we grab our hats and bonnets when the benediction is begun; when it is finished, we shove, so to speak. No frenzy—no fanaticism—no skirmishing; everything perfectly serene. You never see any of us Presbyterians getting in a sweat about religion and trying to massacre the neighbors. Let us all be content with the tried and safe old regular religions, and take no chances on wildcat.

FROM THE *Golden Era*, MARCH 4, 1866.

MORE SPIRITUAL INVESTIGATIONS

I SHALL HAVE this matter of spiritualism "down to a spot," yet, if I do not go crazy in the meantime. I stumbled upon a private fireside seance a night or two ago, where two old gentlemen and a middle-aged gentleman and his wife were communicating (as they firmly believed) with the ghosts of the departed. They have met for this purpose every week for years. They do not "investigate"—they have long since become strong believers, and further investigations are not needed by them. I knew some of these parties well enough to know that whatever deviltry was exhibited would be honest, at least, and that if there were any humbugging done they themselves would be as badly humbugged as any spectator. We kept the investigations going for three hours, and it was rare fun.

They set a little table in the middle of the floor, and set up a dial on it which bore the letters of the alphabet instead of the figures of a clock-face. An index like the minute hand of a clock was so arranged that the tipping of the table would cause it to move around the dial and point to any desired letter, and thus spell words. The lady and two gentlemen sat at the table and rested their hands gently upon it, no other portion of their persons touching it. And the spirits, and some other mysterious agency, came and tilted the table back and forth, sometimes lifting two of its legs three or four inches from the floor and causing the minutehand to travel entirely around the dial. These persons did not move the table themselves; because when no one's hands rested upon it but the lady's it tilted just the same, and although she could have borne down her side of the table, by an effort, it was impossible for her to *lift up her* side with her hands simply resting on top of it. And then the hands of these persons lay perfectly impassable —not rose or fell, and not a tendon grew tense or relaxed as the table tilted—whereas, when they removed their hands and I tilted the table with mine, it required such exertion that muscles and tendons rose and fell and stretched and relaxed with every movement. I do not know who tilted that table, but it was not the medium at any rate. It tired my arms to death merely to spell out four long words on the dial, but thc lady and the ghosts spelled out long conversations without the least fatigue.

The first ghost that announced his presence spelled this on the dial: "My name is Thomas Tilson; I was a preacher. I have been dead many years. I know this man Mark Twain well!"

I involuntarily exclaimed: "The very devil you do?" That old dead parson took me by surprise when he spelled my name, and I felt the cold chills creep over me. Then the ghost and I continued the conversation:

"Did you know me on earth?"

"No. But I read what you write, every day, almost. I like your writings."

"Thank you. But *how* do you read it?—do they take the *Territorial Enterprise* in h— or rather, in heaven, I beg your pardon?"

"No. I read it through my affinity."

"Who is your affinity?"

"Mac Crellish of the *Alta!*"

This excited some laughter, of course—and I will remark here that both ghosts and mediums indulge in jokes, conundrums, doggerel rhymes, and laughter—when the ghost says a good thing he wags the minute hand gaily to and fro to signify laughter.

"Did Mac Crellish ever know you?"

"No. He didn't know me, and doesn't suspect that he is my affinity —but he is, nevertheless. I impress him and influence him every day. If he starts to do what I think he ought not to do, I change his mind."

This ghost then proceeded to go into certain revelations in this connection which need not be printed.

William Thompson's ghost came up. Said he knew me; loved me like a brother; never knew me on earth, though. Said he had been a school teacher in Mott street, New York; was an assistant teacher when he was only fifteen years old, and appeared to take a good deal of pride in the fact. Said he was with me constantly.

"Well," I said, "you get into some mighty bad company sometimes, Bill, if you travel with me." He said it couldn't hurt him.

One of the irrepressible Smiths took the stand, now. He told his name, and said, "I am here!"

"Staunch and true!" said I.

"Colors blue! and liberty forever!" quoth the poetical Smith.

The medium said, "Mr. Smith, Mr. Twain here has been abusing the Smith family—can't you give him a brush?"

And Smith spelled out, "If I only had a brush!" and wagged the minute hand in a furious burst of laughter. Smith thought that was a gorgeous joke. And it might be so regarded in perdition, where Smith lives, but will not excite much admiration here.

Then Smith asked, "Why don't you have some whiskey here?" He was informed that the decanter had just been emptied, Mr. Smith said: "I'll go and fetch some." In about a minute he came back and said: "Don't get impatient—just sit where you are and wait till you see me coming with that whiskey!" and then shook a boisterous laugh on the dial and cleared out. And I supose this old Smarty from h— is going around in the other world yet, bragging about this cheap joke.

A Mr. Wentworth, a very intelligent person for a dead man, came and spelled out a "lecture" of two foolscap pages, on the subject of "Space," but I haven't got space to print it here. It was very beautifully written; the style was smooth, and flowing, the language was well chosen, and the metaphors and similes were apt and very poetical. The only fault I could find about the late Mr. Wentworth's lecture on "Space" was, that there was nothing in it about space. The essayist seemed to be only trying to reconcile people to the loss of friends, by showing that the lost friends were unquestionably in luck in being lost, and therefore should not be grieved for—and the essayist did the thing gracefully and well but devil a word did he say about "Space".

Very well; the *Bulletin* may abuse spiritualism as much as it pleases, but whenever I can get a chance to take a dead and damned Smith by the hand and pass a joke or swap a lie with him, I am going to do it. I am not afraid of such pleasant corpses as these ever running me crazy. I find them better company than a good many live people.

FROM THE *Golden Era*, MARCH 11, 1866.

APPENDIX

BIBLIOGRAPHICAL NOTE

THIS COLLECTION contains all the Mark Twain material to appear in the *Golden Era* during his sojourn in Nevada and California except "Curing a Cold," which is to be found in *Sketches New and Old,* now volume nineteen of *Mark Twain's Works* (Harper and Brothers).

To my knowledge, supplemented by Merle Johnson's listings, thirty of the thirty-eight items here reprinted have never before appeared in book form. The remaining eight have been reprinted incompletely or in volumes beyond the reach of the general reader. A portion of "The Pioneers' Ball" is in *Sketches New and Old.* "Earthquake Almanac," "Among the Spirits," "A Biographical Sketch of George Washington," and "Washoe" under the title "Information for the Million" were included in *The Jumping Frog and Other Sketches* (1867) but were dropped when most of this volume was incorporated in *Sketches New and Old* (1875). In some strange manner "Fitz Smythe's Horse" found its way into *Beadle's Dime Book of Fun, Number 3* (1886). Finally, Kate Milner Rabb used "The Great Prize Fight" and "The Evidence in the Case of Smith vs Jones" in an anthology titled *The Wit and Humor of America* (1907).

The selections in this collection are reprinted in full and without change, except for the correction of typographical errors and the use of paragraphing suited to book rather than newspaper publication.

Printed by
THE WARD RITCHIE PRESS
Los Angeles, California